CU00945677

PREDATOR, PREY

THE BEAST ARISES

Book 1 – I AM SLAUGHTER
Dan Abnett

Book 2 – PREDATOR, PREY
Rob Sanders

Book 3 – THE EMPEROR EXPECTS
Gav Thorpe

Discover the latest books in this multi-volume series at
blacklibrary.com

THE BEAST ARISES

BOOK TWO

PREDATOR, PREY

ROB SANDERS

BLACK LIBRARY

For TC, Jonah and Elliot – you know why…

A BLACK LIBRARY PUBLICATION

First published in Great Britain in 2015 by
Black Library
Games Workshop Ltd
Willow Road
Nottingham NG7 2WS UK

10 9 8 7 6 5 4 3 2 1

Produced by Games Workshop in Nottingham

A CIP record for this book is available from the British Library.

UK ISBN 13: 978 1 78496 123 7
US ISBN 13: 978 1 78496 190 9

See Black Library on the internet at
blacklibrary.com

Find out more about Games Workshop
and the world of Warhammer 40,000 at
games-workshop.com

Printed and bound in China

Fire sputters...
The shame of our deaths
and our heresies is done. They are
behind us, like wretched phantoms. This
is a new age, a strong age, an age of Imperium.
Despite our losses, despite the fallen sons, despite the
eternal silence of the Emperor, now watching over us in
spirit instead of in person, we will endure. There will be no
more war on such a perilous scale. There will be an end
to wanton destruction. Yes, foes will come and
enemies will arise. Our security will be
threatened, but we will be ready, our
mighty fists raised. There will be no
great war to challenge us now.
We will not be brought
to the brink like that
again...

Capturing...

Competition is a universal constant. Territoriality, a quantified given. Empire building – an expectation. The galaxy is quietly expanding, but there will never be enough room for all the species who aspire to its dominion. The appetites of sentient beings tend to the absolute – like our own. This is not base predation. I talk not of the hunter and hunted. This is not survival of the fittest. I have made it my life's work – and that of the life thereafter – to study the grand design of such selection and speciation. It is both wondrous and dreadful.

The apex species of the galaxy compete not for resources or sustenance. They all take more than need demands. They compete because they can. This is intraguild predation, the predators that kill their competitors – the predators that prey on each other. They are the wolves that take down the lion.

We partake in a techno-evolutionary arms race: a galactic test of our suitability to rule, to prosper, to exist. Our success, however, is our failure. With every step we take along the path of enlightenment, dominance and superiority, we plant the seeds of our own destruction. In attempting to annihilate the other sentient species of the galaxy, we force them to adapt. To learn from their mistakes on a genetic level. We create competitors with the evolutionary gifts to wipe us from the face of the known universe.

I think of the terrible things we have achieved. Our countless numbers and culture of conquest. Our forges, our immaterial implementations and the mighty vessels that take our dread weapons to the stars. I think on galactic princes and their gene-sired Legions: our crusaders in the cosmos, our ambassadors of destruction, our lethal gift to enemy empires. I think on these cold considerations... and know that we are doomed.

ONE

Segmentum Solar – rimward sectors

How could it have come to this?

There was little in the way of historical precedent. Invaders announced their intentions with armies and armadas. Some drifted with cruel patience across the void, while others arrived on the edge of our systems with their vessels still frosted from the warp. All were outsiders. They were savage or unreasoning, insatiate or cold in their calculations. They observed humanity's expansion through alien eyes and thought to check its advance. The Imperium became an empire encroached, with the xenos biting at the borders. Alien aggressors took virgin territory a piece at a time or relived histories long past by retaking the ground of their ancients. These were the trials of humanity in a vast and hostile galaxy.

That was before the coming of the Beast.

Early indications of the calamity to come were lost in the devotions and industry of teeming billions. Across hundreds of worlds Imperial citizens went about the drudgery of their existence and servitude, ignorant of the fact that they were being addressed across the void. At first, the noise bursts were swallowed by the vox-static of stars and background radiation. They struggled to make themselves known above the sub-light rumble of charter shipping and the aetherial boom of merchant fleets translating in and out of system. They were lost in the cannon fire of Imperial Navy frigates, engaging pirate fleets on the fringes of frontier space. They were drowned in the industrial undertakings of planetary forges and hive-worlds, in the hymnals echoing about mighty cathedrals and the riotous misery of swarming humanity.

As the noise bursts grew louder and more intense in their infrasonic insistence, the Imperium came to hearken to the herald of their doom. The listeners heard it first: those whose minds and ears were already open. A Navy listening post in the Ourobian Belt. The vox-operators of the 41st Thranxian Rifles on the jungle moon of Bossk. The Izul-11 Telepathica chorale beacon at Cantillus. The rogue trader *Austregal*, operating under a lineal letter of marque in the Wraith Stars. The *Austregal* was authorised to prey on the ghostships of the Zahr-Tann craftworld, but had discovered that the xenos had mysteriously moved out of the segmentum.

Credit for official recognition of the phenomenon on the Inner Rim was shared, however. At the same time that Divisio Linguistica adept Mobian Ortrex isolated the content of the noise bursts on the Ark Mechanicus vessel *Singularitii*, Sister-Emeritus Astrid of the Schola-Lexicon translated a vox-capture of the anomaly at the Mount Nisei Seminarium.

They swiftly and separately came to the same conclusion and communicated their findings to Imperial authorities across the rimward sectors with equal urgency.

What sounded like the kind of belly-thunder that might erupt from a carnivorous death world predator was in fact a savage xenos vernacular. A barbaric decree from a tyrant species, hollered impossibly across the void. The words were raw and delivered like a barrage of artillery, but they were unmistakably greenskin. The broadcast assumed myriad forms, although certain linguistic patterns were the most repeated. The translation was crude but compelling.

Amongst the barbaric abandon of mindless monstrosity, the being announced itself as 'the Slaughter to come' and 'the Beast'. It was beside itself with brutality and promised 'blood for blood', 'an end to weakling empires' and 'the stench of oblivion'.

As the rimward sectors of the Segmentum Solar would come to understand, the Beast made good on its promises. The noise bursts spread. Within a few Terran standard weeks, the six outlying systems reporting the phenomenon became sixty. In mere days it became six hundred. The Beast spoke. The people listened. What had previously been distant thunder, unacknowledged and ignored, broke above the heads of the Emperor's subjects. Across the worlds of the rimward sectors, the mind-splitting roar of the Beast became everything. Humanity could not function. People could not work; they could not sleep; they could not think. Schedules were disrupted. Tithes went unmet. Order began to slip from the Imperium's gauntleted grasp.

Millions descended into madness. The grim rigidity of

humanity's tyrannised existence – harsh and imbalanced as it was – actually served to protect the masses from the threat of the outsider. Most Imperial citizens had never set foot outside their habsteads or districts, let alone left their home worlds. Apart from a small number of surviving veterans from the Astra Militarum, very few people had actually seen a member of a xenos race. So when the unbridled rage of an alien monstrosity unfolded in their minds, many simply didn't have the mental fortitude to hold onto their sanity.

Amid the collapse of structures and the riotous descent of planets into chaos, there were some who heard the Beast reach out to them – and they reached back. Something repressed and downtrodden found expression in the alien rancour. Unlike the God-Emperor, who – apart from in the chapel and catechism – seemed strangely absent from the life of the average Imperial, the Beast was there. Its fury was present between their temples. It echoed about their streets. It rumbled through the void above their home worlds. It didn't take long for shrines to be defaced and missions to be torched, as the faithless found their way to a nihilistic comfort in the doom to come.

There is power in words, but more so in deeds. The Beast made a shocking impression on the billions of the rimward sectors with its roaring menace, but then came the gravity storms. If the Beast's emerging acolytes desired more evidence of the being's almighty power, they needed to look no further than its unseen mastery of destructive force.

While the augur banks of sprint traders, research stations and fabricator moons detected and monitored the gravitic anomalies afflicting the segmentum margins, many only came to know of their presence through the cataclysmic events unfolding about them. The Angelini Hub dockyards – a modern wonder of the Imperium, orbiting the great mercantile world of Korsicus IV like a belt – simply shattered. An endeavour that had taken more than a thousand years to engineer and accrete drifted off into the void in splintered fragments, along with the bodies of the million or so merchant traders and their families that called the Angelini Hub home. For the common Imperial citizen, there was no explanation for such a tragedy. Mechanicus adepts and the Hub's Naval security had next to no idea what had caused the gravity storm. For most, it was simply a demonstration of the Beast's power and potential.

On the low-gravity world of Virgilia, where the lofty towers of schola and universitae reached for the heavens and pierced the clouds, the anomaly wreaked havoc. The collegia world passed through an erupting gravity well, causing the planet to violently wobble. Like a slow-motion holo-pict, the forest of hightowers, spires and belfries came crashing down on the ancient colleges and institutes below. Within minutes, the cloud-piercing skyline had become a dust-cloaked silhouette of finely crafted rubble.

World after decimated world fell before the might of the gravity storms. Fenimore had the misfortune of orbiting the gas giant 88-Clavia. Usually the inhabitants of the moon enjoyed the sight of the giant's beautiful ring system in their sky. After the anomaly tore through the delicate arrangement, however, death rained down on Fenimore from above. Shards of ice and long-shattered shepherd moons sliced down through the thin skies and cut the screaming population to bloody ribbons. As the world turned, night became day and the dawn ushered in the razor-storm.

On the fortress-world of Brigantia III, General Milus Montague of the 47th Heavy Columnus had two million Imperial Guardsmen amassing for a push on the Zodiox Rift – including honoured regiments of the Phaxatine-of-Foot and Droonian Longshanks. The sparse systems of the Rift had become a petri dish of alien infestations: the Hrud, the Noulia and the Chromes. The xenos filth lived to spread their contagion another day, however. As something colossal attempted to break through into the reality of the Brigantia System, the fortress-world trembled and then succumbed to unseen and unimaginable gravitic pressures. Despite its bastions, armour formations and millions of Guardsmen, Brigantia III had no defence against the intrusion of another world.

The planet exploded. As gargantuan chunks of fortress-world rocketed away, demolishing the flotillas of super-heavy troop transports and Navy escorts waiting to receive General Montague's Zodiox crusade force in orbit, another planet had taken its place. A small, black moon: one of many appearing throughout the sectors of the Inner Rim like bad omens.

Amongst the calamitous roaring of the Beast and the gravitic disasters afflicting worlds, these unnatural satellites materialised across the rimward sectors. The heralds of catastrophe, they ripped through reality to take their place among the ornamental orbs of busy Imperial systems. Some were black like coal, eating up the light reflected off nearby stars and planets. The surfaces of others were a collage of wreckage and plating, rusted into an armoured shell. The rock monstrosity above Arx II Antareon bore a colossal clan glyph painted across its ugly face, while the attack moon rising over desert world of Sanveen was a mechanical horror – a patchwork metal skull grinning down on the doomed Imperial citizenry with alien drollery.

Praxedes Prime was one of the first recorded worlds to experience the attack moons' gargantuan weapons. Gravity beams struck the shrine world's surface, chewing though the sovereign city states and tearing temples, basilicae and cathedrals violently skywards. Light years away, Port Oberon – a fleet base situated near a busy subsector ether-nexus – was pulverised. Colossal rocks, meteorites and planetary chunks, vomited forth from gaping launch craters in the pock-marked surface of a materialising attack moon, smashed through stationed sentry cruisers and fleeing merchant shipping.

The worst was to come, however. As well as rocketing projectiles and graviton beams, the attack moons unleashed plagues of ramshackle gunships, salvage hulks and rammers that enveloped escaping vessels in a web of grapnels and gunfire. Survivors on victim worlds climbed out from the wreckage of demolished cities, their eyes fixed on the slaughter above and the attack moons glowering down on them. They watched until their skies grew black – black with the swarms of descending rocks, landers and greenskin capsules. Oblivion beckoned.

This was not the first time the Inner Rim had suffered greenskin attacks. In recent memory, the Archfiend of Urswine had led its invasion into Subsector Borodino. The orks poured into the Grange Worlds like a green tide. Their decimation of the agri-world crops and tenders brought the nearby hive-world of Quora Coronis to the brink of starvation. It took the best part of a decade for the Coronida 3rd through 9th Indentured and the Royal Borodino 'Blues' to drive the Archfiend and its splintering horde back to its degenerate empire.

The Beast was not the Archfiend of Urswine, however. The Archfiend's invasion force, while a savage sea of green into which Imperial worlds went to die, were mere runts compared to the Beast's hulking monsters. Amongst the Beast's countless number, the Urswine orks would have been trampled under foot. Even the greatest of the Archfiend's brutes – perhaps even the Archfiend itself – would have been lost in the shadow of the Beast's invader savages. The puniest of the Beast's monsters were small mountains of muscle, standing snaggle-jaw and shoulder over other orks. Striding through the mobs and madness were greater beasts still: towers of tusk, green flesh and ferocity. Like gargants or giant effigies of greenskin gods brought to life, these hulks carried colossal weapons that demolished buildings at a single strike and monstrous guns that mangled infantry and tank formations with equal, bloody ease.

This was the gift the Beast brought to each planet on the Inner Rim of the Segmentum Solar: an apocalyptic flood of alien wrath. World by world, the Imperium began to fall, drowning in innocent blood less spilled than splattered. No subsector escaped armageddon. No star cluster survived the Beast. Wherever the black doom of attack moons appeared, life ended: the crowded worlds of the Scinta Stars, the void colonies of Constantin Thule, the Skull Nebula, the Gastornis Marches, planets along the Carcasion Flux, the Quatra Sound and Imperial strongholds on the Neo-Tavius Drift – even the quarantined worlds of the Prohibited Zone and the marauder-haunted reaches of wilderness space were sacrificed to feed the Beast's apparently insatiable appetite for annihilation.

Billions perished in the fires of the invasion's ire. Worlds lay smashed. The people prayed for an intervention – but none came. Astra Militarum forces and planetary defences stationed in the path of ruin did what they could, but were swiftly overrun. No reinforcements were sent. No reclamation fleet from Ancient Terra was on its way. Only death worlds and Adeptus Astartes home worlds seemed to have the resilience to slow the invasion's progress. From individual planets, the Beast's alien ambitions grew to the destruction of subsectors. From those, the green plague spread – overwhelming entire sectors of Imperial space. From prayer, the people turned to raw hope. Like the Archfiend's feuding clans, perhaps the Beast's monstrosities would tire, fragment and fall to fighting between themselves.

But as the months went by in misery and slaughter, it became apparent that this Beast was something else. A new breed of xenos savage. It would not stop. It would never stop. From subsector to sector it would lead its barbarian horde – and from there corewards, until the entirety of Segmentum Solar belonged to the greenskin race and Ancient Terra was clutched in the Beast's filthy alien claw.

TWO

Undine – Hive Tyche

Lux Allegra could not believe what she was seeing.

The commander had been in the underhive for a number of days. Her mission had been simple: locate the Lord Governor and get him to safety. With the hive-world of Undine going to hell about them – hivers rioting, communities flooding, hundreds of thousands trapped under collapsing accretia and rubble – it seemed ironic that she, a former ganger, should be the one selected to lead the rescue. That Lux Allegra, who had lived so long by the edge of her knives and the whim of the ocean currents, should be chosen to pull the bastard blue-bloods out.

As underhiver and pirate, she had robbed the Lord Governor and his hive of monies and supplies. She had outrun his pirate-hunters, his enforcers and Maritine Guard. That was before she had been caught, press-ganged and promoted, however. Now *she* wore the hated uniform: the beret and the blue-and-white stripe, the flak plate and pads.

'Why me, sir?' Allegra had put to General Phifer. 'Surely

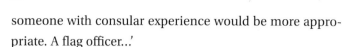

someone with consular experience would be more appropriate. A flag officer...'

'Stop apologising for what you're not,' the general had grizzled back. 'I don't need somebody to hold the Governor's cloak tails.'

Everyone knew where the Beacon Spire was. As both pirate and commander, Allegra had used the rotating lamps of the lantern palace to navigate the shantipelagos and hazards of sunken architecture on the seaward approach to Hive Tyche. Few others among the Undine 41st Maritine would have been able to navigate their way down through the city's crumbling levels and sub-strata, and Chief Gohlandr and the twenty Maritine Guard under her command had been glad of her knowledge and assurance. With the Beacon Spire landing pad destroyed, along with the mighty plasma lamps themselves, and the lantern palace collapsing about them, Allegra had been forced to take them down.

The seas had quaked. The island hives had shaken. The Lord Governor – aged and infirm – had to be ripped from his pipes, tubes and wheeled throne. Carried between two valets, it would have been difficult enough to get the aristocrat out. Artemus Borghesi refused to leave, however, without the menagerie of extended family and hangers-on who had rushed to the spire palace for safety. With these, the patriarch included the palace servants and pets. While Allegra had been glad of the extra guns in the form of the ceremonial spire guardians, she had Chief Gohlandr shoot the Lord Governor's retinue of prize flippered marine mammals – just to end the argument. Even then, the emaciated Borghesi forced the rescue party to wait while he had his valets dress him in his old fleet dress uniform, complete with medals and bicorne hat.

'It just doesn't seem appropriate,' Allegra had told the general. 'I'm of the Brethren. I've robbed, pillaged and stolen from this man and his spirekin.'

'And now I want you to steal him away,' Phifer had insisted. 'The extraction will be hot: the transport will get to you where it can, but you may have to improvise...'

With her Marineers leading the way with their assault lasrifles, Allegra escorted the mob of inbreeds and palace favourites down through the stairwells of factoria and hab levels, down into the derelict underhive. An evacuation from the aerie villa terraces had to be abandoned, due to the shuttle being overwhelmed by swarms of terrified hivers. The pick-up became ugly, with the shuttle being rushed and crashing into the spire wall. The mob turned on the Maritine Guard and Allegra was forced to order Imperial civilians shot, just to keep the madness at bay. A second lift simply didn't happen. Allegra had instructed Chief Gohlandr to establish a perimeter amongst the sky talons and gigabarge dry docks. There they had joined forces with Commandant Hektor Szekes and five of his enforcers in their black carapace armour. Forced to abandon their precinct house due to rioting and gangs emboldened by the chaos, the enforcers had been fighting running battles through the freightstacks.

Hours overdue and faced with small armies of trigger-happy gangers driven up though the sub-levels by flooding, Allegra ordered the Marineers and their charges on. The commander had little choice but to push down through the underhive and out through the pontoon shanties. There were fewer gangers taking potshots at the Marineers and enforcers, but the sub-levels were filling with rising seawater and some sections were now fully submerged. Gravity quakes collapsed tunnels both before and behind them, sending torrents of floodwater through the depths that swept away several of their number.

Borghesi had struggled. The Lord Governor had seen more of his Hive-Primus in the last two-score hours than the trecentigenarian had experienced in his elongated life. Even carried by his valets, the physical demands of the descent were too much for him. Combined with the overexcitement of riots and gunfire, the extraction meant to save Artemus Borghesi's life almost took it on several occasions. Every few levels brought on a fresh attack of organ-failure and the personal physicians Borghesi had insisted on including in their party had to resuscitate the mouldering aristocrat.

'I'm not saying you need to lay on the airs and graces, commander,' Phifer had said, 'but the man is the planetary governor: the God-Emperor's representative on this world. I don't care how hurt his sensibilities are but I need you to get him out of there alive and in one piece. Understood?'

The commander had nodded. The commander had saluted. It was less simple than that in the hive. For two days the Marineers navigated a labyrinthine hell of flooded darkness, losing a number of the grandee's frail relatives to the rigours of exposure and exhaustion. The vox-channels kept Allegra apprised regarding the impossibilities of a planetary invasion that she could not see. Across her headset, in the dripping gloom of the depths, the insanity and slaughter reported and described seemed distant and unreal. It was unnerving, regardless. Allegra kept her men focused on the mundane: reconnaissance, the conservation of power and keeping the master-vox and the power packs of their lasrifles as dry as possible. When Chief Gohlandr blasted the rusted lock mechanism from the maintenance opening and kicked open the metal cover, water flowed out while daylight flooded in. Leading the way with her laspistol and shielding her eyes, the commander stepped out on the rockcrete.

What she experienced made her want to return to the cold and dark of the claustrophobic underhive. It was horrific.

Lux Allegra could not believe what she was seeing.

THREE

Undine – the Pontoon Shanties

It was raining meteorites. Large meteorites. Allegra watched the incandescent rocks – too many to count – stream from the sky. The heavens were a thatch-work of crossing dust trails, while the air trembled with the sonic boom of descents. Staring out across the chromatic water, Allegra could see the distant silhouette of Hive Galatae: mist-cloaked, massive and falling into the polluted sea. Hive Tyche may have been the Hive-Primus but Galatae was older and bigger, and like the capital, Hive Galatae had suffered the gravity quakes and disturbances. Vast tidal waves had done for Hives Arethusa and Thetis, but it was the trembling seabed and ruptured hydrothermics that toppled great Galatae.

Above the ghost of the falling hive a new moon had risen over the ocean hive-world of Undine, a black and impossible thing that held its ugly station above the planet. Its cratered surface made it appear as though it had a misshapen face: two eyes, one larger than the other, and a crooked valley-fracture for a nose. Its southern hemisphere was delineated by the iron glint of a colossal metal jaw fixed to the moon's circumference. Allegra had seen alien brutes wear such contraptions in place of jaws torn from their monstrous faces. Terrified hivers were calling it the trap-jaw moon.

'Commander...'

As suggested by the flooded underhive, sea levels had risen with the gravitic perversions. The hive's island foundations had been buried beneath the chemical cocktail that was Undine's oceans, and the pontoon shanties – smashed and tangled with weed – had risen to cluster-shunt about the hive walls. Beyond, the meteorites were hammering the ocean surface. Great eruptions of water and spray marked their landings before their great weight contributed to their continued descent.

Watching several of the nearest splash-impacts, the commander came to realise that they weren't all streaming rocks. Some were armour-plated pods and capsules. An invasion had begun in overwhelming earnest. Without great Undine herself inviting the alien savages into her dark ocean-world depths, the monsters would already have swamped the planet. Allegra watched as the engine-mounted asteroids and junker pods carried their raging xenos payloads down below the waves.

'Commander!'

Stumbling around and looking up the shell-face of the hive, Allegra saw that the spire had been demolished. Feathered sea-raptors swooped and dived in search of their missing nests. Allegra turned again, and then she saw them.

Scrambling out of the shallows in a constant stream, like

the unkillable bastards they were, were thousands of hulking orks. Their skin glistened wet over their fearful brawn and their beady eyes were red with unreasoning alien rage. Like the starved vermin of the stars, they clambered and swarmed. The greenskin beasts hauled themselves up the tottering architecture and busy accretia of the city's shell. They scrambled over each other – the mass of claws, arms and jaws snapping and scraping its way upwards like a living geyser of green flesh, gushing its way up the hive wall. Greater beasts still mounted the writhing column of muscle, climbing monstrously over their xenos kin. Beetle-backed landers, belching black smoke, hovered at the cavernous mouths of rocket-mauled entry points. There they delivered further mobs of monstrous brutality and ork chieftains buried in exoskeletal suits of plate and piston. They could smell the herds of terror-stricken humanity hiding within the byzantine dereliction of the hive. They climbed. They roared. The Beast bawled its fury through the combined thunder of their barrel chests.

'Lux!' Chief Gohlandr shouted. The intimacy of first names brought the commander back from the breathtaking dread of the spectacle.

'Chief,' Allegra barked back. 'Establish a perimeter – our backs to the wall.'

She looked to the dribble of minor aristocrats and hangers-on stumbling out into the daylight. There were no words to describe the horror on their powdered faces. As members of the Undine 41st Maritine splashed down into the shallows at the chief's bawling order, Allegra called out, 'Gunner DuDeq!'

The gunner fell out of line, his lasrifle snug at his chin, his eye staring down his sights at the greenskin hordes about them. Holding her pistol upright, Allegra stepped behind the gunner and cranked the master-vox that DuDeq was humping on his back. Snatching an ear-horn and hailer from the pack, she shouted above the roar of the beasts and waves. '*Capricorn-Six, Capricorn-Six* – this is Commander Allegra, respond.'

Allegra waited as Lyle Gohlandr splashed forwards with his gunners, assuming positions about the commander and Lord Governor amongst the wet and busy architecture. '*Capricorn-Six*,' she persisted, 'this is Commander Allegra with the Undine Forty-First, "Screeching Eagles".'

The xenos were everywhere. Allegra watched as monstrous multitudes emerged from the water, hauling themselves up out of waves. 'We have acquired our target and are awaiting evacuation. Our position is three fifty-four fifty-two fifty-six: Primus north by north-east. Do you read, *Capricorn*?'

The green bastards swarming all over the architecture could see them. Allegra felt their blood-vision, their appetite, their need to smash and kill. Like rivers diverting and changing direction, the hordes came for them: hundreds upon hundreds of leathery beasts thundering up through the surf, rounding an artificial headland created by the domed roof of a freight-barbican and skidding down through the grotesques and gargoyles of shell-stone decoration. They ran at them like things of madness, all bared tooth and tusk.

Allegra searched for hope. High above them, gunships and assault carriers were drifting about the hive-heights, exchanging fire with the enemy swarms. Something big fired back from within the penetrated city shell, turning one of the aircraft into a tumbling fireball of death and wreckage. Out on the water, amongst the raining rocks and pods, was a Maritine cutter, its prow-mounted inferno cannon bathing the shoreline masses in a stream of flame.

Two shallow-hulled landing craft hit hive-city masonry further along the chemical coast. Their prow-ramps crashed down into the surf and platoons of Maritine Guard stormed up towards the dripping greenskins. Allegra saw the constellations of las-fire. She watched as the grim determination of the soldiers' faces fell to fearful dread. Like the water washing back and forth up the shorelines, throngs of greenskin predators, newly risen from the depths, turned and thundered back at the shallows. The las-fire intensified. The landing faltered. Marineers began stumbling back towards their craft, but nothing could save them. Drawn by the panic and the screams, surrounding monsters ran at the butchery, hacking limbs and bodies apart.

'*Capricorn-Six...*' Allegra half-pleaded.

'They're not coming,' Chief Gohlandr roared over the din. 'Permission to open fire?'

After days of power conservation, Allegra gave her men the order. 'Fire at will.'

The perimeter became a halo of scintillation. With power packs hot to the touch and lasrifles unleashing beam-snaps at full automatic, the Maritine gunners made their stand. The greenskins didn't care. Their armour scraps and iron-hard flesh soaked up the curtain of light. Riddled bodies, searing and smoking, were stamped into the masonry by the racing hordes. Beasts barged and clawed at each other in primal desperation to be the first to land a kill. Fire from the guardsmen's rifles was punctuated by flash of the spire guardians' fusils and the repetitive *pump-crash* of the enforcers' shotguns.

'Chief!' Allegra called.

'I know!' he barked back, but he hadn't seen it. He hadn't heard it. Amongst the cacophony of the brutes bearing down on his position and the drumming of his rapidly-emptying assault rifle, the chief hadn't noticed the whine of approaching aircraft.

'No,' Allegra shouted, adding to the barrage a stream of las-bolts from her pistol. 'Look.'

Dropping out of the sky were a trio of Thunderbolt fighter-bombers. They were zeroing in on the hive, coming in low and fast – which could mean only one thing. They were going to cleanse the shoreline.

'Fall back!' Allegra called. 'Gunners – fall back!'

Allegra waved the Lord Governor's valets and inbreeds back through the maintenance opening. Tearing DuDeq back with her by his vox-pack, the commander backed with them. The chief finally clocked the approaching Thunderbolts and echoed Allegra's order.

Most of the Marineers didn't need an excuse to run from the closing wall of blades, gaping barrels and green flesh. Some, like Gunners Friel and LaNoy, couldn't make themselves move. Whether it was fear or faith in their weapons, the guardsmen remained, burning streams of light into the rabid ranks. They were gone in moments. Swallowed by the horde. There was no gallant defence. No sweeping bladework with broad bayonet or cutlass. The guardsmen were shreds in seconds.

As Chief Gohlandr pushed the last of the Marineers into the maintenance opening, Allegra saw the roaring masses behind him accelerate up the rockcrete. The greenskins did not heed the Thunderbolts screeching overhead. They did not see the mountain range of flame erupting up the shoreline behind them. Gohlandr, Allegra and Commandant Szekes slammed the opening cover shut. The hammer of claws on the metal was almost immediate and the cover was briefly wrenched back open, before the Marineers were suddenly thrown back as a blast of overpressure from outside hurled it closed again. About them the darkness of the tunnel quaked as the airstrike ripped its way up the shore. The scratching and frenetic thunder of fists on the metal covering died away, swallowed in the apocalyptic howl of destruction.

Eyes glinted by the light of the few lamps the Marineers had left. Precious moments passed. The enforcer commandant went to open the cover.

'Wait!' Allegra ordered, drifting her ear towards the hot metal. Satisfied, she nodded. The enforcer went to barge the covering open with one carapace-armoured shoulder, but it all but fell off its roasted hinges.

Smoke was swiftly clearing with the onshore breeze. As the soot and ash whirled in the wind Allegra stepped out, onto charred bodies. The shoreline was carpeted with blackened xenos corpses. The commander found herself nodding with satisfaction, but she knew the beasts would be back – and in number. Offshore, Allegra could see a few remaining guardsmen swamped by orks who were overrunning their battered landing craft. The Maritine cutter that the commander had also been pinning her hopes on was now listing horribly as some greenskin titan seized it from below. About the craft, the pontoon shanties – in chaotic disarray – had fragmented and were floating away from one another in ramshackle sections. The shoreline was overrun and the absence of their assigned evacuation had been a blow, but Allegra couldn't afford to wait any longer. The Screeching Eagles simply couldn't hold the perimeter.

'The pontoons,' the commander ordered. 'Make for the pontoons.'

Directing the remaining guardsmen into two columns, Gohlandr barked at the Lord Governor and his freakish retinue to run into the shallows. Many of the spireborns had never been near the waters for fear of pollutant contamination. They were not keen on stumbling into the chemical shallows, but the heart-stopping vision of green fiends stomping up through the cadavers of their monster-kin lent the aristocrats resolve. Cutting a path through the surf with savage bursts of las-fire and lobbed frag grenades, Gohlandr led the way through the hazards of emerging orks.

Clambering up the side of a pontoon platform bearing part of the shattered shanty, the chief took the frail Lord Governor from his exhausted valets and hauled him up onto the amphibious community. As the Marineers and their charges climbed aboard, shanty wretches emerged from hiding. They extended emaciated arms and skeletal hands to help the screaming survivors – survivors they did not know were their palace-dwelling betters.

Like some death world reptile, a hulking greenskin tramped up the scorched shoreline towards the fleeing rescue party. It towered above the other examples of its species that were swarming up the coast. The creature grizzled to itself as it smashed the monstrous weapon it was heaving with a frustrated fist. It shook the rotor-cannon, and water cascaded from the barrels.

Another savage shake and the weapon stuttered to reluctant life. The unexpected eruption of shells tore through the unfortunate greenskins in front before the creature angled its fire up the shore and cut the rescue party in half. With the shallows thrashing and spitting in the gunfire, Allegra fell forwards into the sea.

She was only below the surface for a few seconds but as she emerged she felt her eyes burn and her skin sear from the chemicals in the water. Finding her way back to her feet, she started wading back towards the shore. Commandant Szekes and a handful of guardsmen had been cut off by the wall of bullets unleashed by the advancing beast.

'Commander!' Lyle Gohlandr roared. There was nothing she could do, but she couldn't bring herself to turn her back on her men. It was over quickly. Greenskins bounded through desperate las-fire to maul the Undine Marineers. Szekes blasted through several thuggish creatures before his combat shotgun ran empty. Throwing the weapon at an ork bulldozing its way at him, the enforcer drew his crackling power maul; but as he readied himself to bury the weapon in the creature's domed skull, he did not see a larger monster cannon through the advancing ranks behind him.

The beast smashed the enforcer to the side with one

swing of its brute hammer. Szekes' broken body landed some distance away in a mound of bloody bones and torn carapace. The sight brought Allegra to her senses and she turned, striding through the shallows for the drifting shanty.

Helped up onto the pontoon by one of the Lord Governor's spire guardians, Allegra looked up, searching for Chief Gohlandr. Greenskins were clambering up the rusted metal drums and flotation tanks, only to meet the barrels of assault lasrifles pointing down at them. A number broke through and charged wildly about the corrugated habs, multi-shacks and hovels, but were blasted off-board by the two remaining enforcers. The pontoon shanty was floating away from the hive, but not nearly fast enough. The blood-splattered landing craft now belonged to the orks, and the cutter was sinking. The monstrous greenskin that had done for the vessel was aflame; there was fire on the water, with the inferno cannon's ruptured tanks bleeding promethium across the surface of the sea. With the craft conquered, the beast disappeared below the flickering waves, dousing its flame-tangled form.

The Thunderbolts were banking for another run and orks were leaping from the blasted city-shell. Flailing green bodies tumbled the lethal distance to the roofs and rockcrete below. Some creatures made it, however, latching on to drifting gunships and carriers with claws and brute prosthetics, before smashing though into the cockpits and bringing the aircraft down. Worst of all, the hive was drowning in alien filth. Like a rampant mould growing up the city walls, greenskins were swarming the shell, rabid and unstoppable. The pontoon shanty would share a similar fate.

A beast erupted from the water like a carnivorous fish, its jaws snapping. Pulling hard on the trigger, Allegra unloaded the rest of her power pack into the thing's face. Another had torn through the rickety walkway and was cannoning towards her. Las-bolts from nearby guardsman plucked at the monster, but did little to stop it. The patchwork floor bounced with its footsteps. Dropping the empty pistol and grabbing the wobbly support, Allegra leapt the rail, allowing the creature to thunder past.

Just as she was about to climb back, a meaty claw grabbed her by the leg. An ork had her. She could feel the feral fury in its grip, its filthy fist enclosing the whole of her booted calf. It hauled itself up to meet her, its tusk-thronged maw mumbling some alien insanity. Allegra snatched for the only weapon she had left: her officer's hanger. It was a polite weapon, nothing like the brute blades she used in her former life. Its single monomolecular edge was serviceable, however, and cleared its stubby scabbard with oiled ease. The blade slashed though the greenskin's exposed throat, giving even the mindless monster pause. It released her and with the sole of her boot against its cavernous chest she pushed it back into the water with a grunt.

As she climbed up onto the pontoon shanty, the commander felt the structure lurch. A rock or capsule had plunged into the water nearby, rocking the section and knocking several terrified inhabitants into the water. It wasn't stopping the greenskins, however, who were surfacing from sinking pods and descent craft and climbing up the nearest structures they could find.

'Lux!' she heard as she wiped and resheathed her bloody

hanger. It was Gohlandr. The chief was on a bent and rusty balcony above, tangled in washing lines and rags. Gunner DuDeq was with him, and the Lord Governor's skeletal arm was draped across the vox-officer's shoulder. Gohlandr dropped DuDeq's assault rifle down to Allegra and she caught it in both hands. She called up to him.

'Get Borghesi higher,' she ordered.

'What about you?' the chief roared back over the chaos.

'I'm coming,' she told him. Checking the lasrifle's depleted power pack and priming it to fire on full automatic, Allegra shouldered the weapon and began a messy climb of the shanty structure.

Two floors up, and the profusion of purchase offered by the ramshackle hab-shacks and walkways allowed the commander to make good progress. Occasionally, she hooked her flak armour on protruding struts or exposed rivets of the structure. In the background she could still hear the bark of enforcer shotguns and the staccato drum of las-bolts above. Greenskins, frothing at the maw, had made equally economic climbs and were savaging the dwindling party of guardsmen and survivors making their way up through the shanty. Risking a glance below, Allegra saw that the pontoon levels were completely overrun. Like Hive Tyche, the shanty had succumbed to the greenskin swarms.

The structure suddenly staggered, knocking Allegra from her precarious purchase. This wasn't the shockwave from a plunging rock or pod: something had hit the shanty. Her arm slipped out of her rifle strap. She snatched for the stock, and dangled from the lasgun's pistol grip by one hand. The strap had been caught on a rusted nail. As the shanty rocked, Allegra bounced off the corrugated wall of a shack.

A greenskin – black, scarred and charred – had surfaced like a behemoth and punched through the pontoon hull of the shanty. As water cascaded from its gargantuan body, the beast swept derelict shacks and habs aside with one furious arm, knocking mobs of its own xenos kin back into the shallows. One monster had the rabid audacity to roar its frustration, and the larger beast snatched it up in one titanic claw and snapped its carping head clean off its shoulders.

Reaching up for the rifle with her other hand, Allegra found her way back to hand- and boot-holds on the shanty wall. Slipping the blessed rifle back over her shoulder, the commander climbed for her life, with the greenskin starting its own shanty-listing ascent behind her.

The chief had reached the topmost hovels. In imitation of the hive cities they emulated, the highest habshacks boasted the most room and even welded terrace-overhangs. They were like palaces compared to the corrugated coffins below. Gohlandr and the remaining Marineers were sending a storm of light down at the monstrous creature. Climbing up onto a creaking walkway, Allegra took her assault rifle and buried the stock in one shoulder. She could not allow the greenskin to reach the upper levels. It had not yet noticed her, the colossal ork's attention remaining firmly on its infuriated ascent and the stabbing burn of las-beams into its already roasted flesh.

Leaning into the rifle, the commander started to hammer the green, uncooked flesh of the beast's exposed belly. The searing wound eventually got the monster's attention and it brought the full ugliness of its scorch-smeared face and blackened tusks down to the walkway.

'That's right,' Allegra spat, sending a fresh volley of fire into the beast's melted maw. 'On me, you bastard. On me!'

The giant greenskin took the bait and roared a foetid gale of flesh-breath at the commander. One huge fist smashed through the walkway. Allegra felt the wire mesh beneath her boots disappear, and instinctively turned and clawed for the collapsing walkway. Her fingers found grating and she clung on, allowing her rifle to drop with the debris. The beast had not only knocked out the walkway; its fist had ripped away the entire corner section of the shanty-level. Crawling up to where the walkway was barely hanging onto the collage-walls, Allegra saw that the destruction had revealed the structure's innards. A little slum-girl sat in the corner of her hovel, her eyes wide and white against the dirty mask of her terrified face. Allegra stared from the girl to the greenskin. The monster waded inwards through the dilapidated wreckage, forcing its mangled face through the jury-rigged architecture.

'Here,' Allegra soothed, opening her arms to the small, stricken child. The girl didn't move. The greenskin monstrosity was a nightmare spectacle that demanded her full attention.

'Now!' the commander roared. There wasn't time for assuaging comforts. The creature closed. The child ran – straight into Allegra's arms.

'Hold on,' she told the child, as the slum-girl wrapped her arms around Allegra's neck and clung to her back. Allegra stepped up onto the walkway rail and began climbing for the shanty-stack. A monstrous growl built up within the great greenskin and echoed about the dereliction before the beast withdrew itself from the ruined structure.

Allegra felt the rumble of the monster's movements on the other side of the accretion. She climbed for all she was worth, with the child hanging from her back.

'Chief?' she called up at the terrace. But he was nowhere to be seen. 'Anybody?' The gunfire had stopped also. Allegra began to imagine the worst. Gohlandr and the rescue party dead. Greenskins waiting for her at the end of an exhausting climb.

The monster ork was suddenly there beside her. Both commander and child were suddenly enveloped in the thing's bestial roar of triumph as it clawed its way around the corner of the shanty.

'Lyle!' Allegra screamed, but there wasn't anyone above her. The beast reached out for her.

The shanty-stack shook with sudden violence. The gargantuan greenskin was lost in a raging fireball. As the flame evaporated and the black cloud cleared, Allegra saw the waspish outline of a Maritine Guard gunship drift clear. Its nosecone flashed with the revolving barrels of its gatling cannon. The greenskin monster, its back flayed of flesh from the gunship's rocket attack and drowning in fresh flames, retreated back around the corner, away from the punishing cannon fire.

Stunned by the explosion and with her ears still aching from the blast, Allegra scrambled up the last few levels of the shanty accretion. A few agonising moments from the top she found Gohlandr and Gunner DuDeq. They were saying something, but she couldn't make it out. As they hauled her and the child up onto the scrap-metal terrace, she saw *Capricorn-Six* hovering just above and Undine Maritine Guard helping the Lord Governor and what remained of his inbred family aboard. DuDeq went to take the child but the girl wouldn't let go, instead crawling around to the commander's flak-armoured front.

'It's okay,' she said as Gohlandr helped her towards the Valkyrie carrier. Only a few of her men remained – grim-faced but glad to see their commander. One of Szekes' enforcers had made it also, surrounded by a cluster of terrified slummers and urchins Gohlandr had picked up on their ascent through the shanty-stack.

An officer jogged down the ramp and saluted Allegra. He introduced himself.

'Lieutenant Kale.'

'What?'

'Lieutenant Kale,' the officer repeated. 'I have orders to take you and the Lord Governor to the general.'

Allegra nodded and went to step on board.

'I'm not cleared for unauthorised civilians,' the lieutenant said, indicating the child in the commander's arms and the shanty folk staring up at them, waiting to be slaughtered by climbing greenskins.

Allegra went to reply but a voice from behind beat her to it.

'Let the hivers aboard.'

As Lieutenant Kale turned, Allegra saw Lord Governor Borghesi, strapped into a stretcher. 'That's an order, lieutenant.'

'Yes, sir,' Kale replied, ordering his Marineers to admit the wretches.

Lux Allegra collapsed against the troop bay wall with the little girl still in her arms. She felt *Capricorn-Six* ascend, leaving the pontoon shanty to the rabid swarms of green-skins, and carry them high up into the Undinian skies. She felt the assault carrier bank from side to side as it negoti-ated the ork capsules and rocks raining from the heavens. Chief Gohlandr allowed his flak-armoured back to slide down the bay wall opposite. He watched Allegra with the slummer girl and found his way to a grizzled smile.

Allegra smiled back. She enjoyed the moment of calm. The feeling of safety. The last few days had been a night-marish hell. She'd found Borghesi as she had been ordered and got him out of the hive. As the odds had grown against them and as the alien apocalypse engulfed Undine, Allegra came to realise that she had not fought her way through the city, negotiated the flooded underhive and fled the burning shore because of orders. She had fought to survive – just like she had always done. Somewhere along the way, she came to realise that it was no longer her survival that mat-tered. It wasn't even the survival of the child in her arms, freshly plucked from calamity.

It was the child growing in her belly. Lyle Gohlandr's child. The pair stared at each other across the beautiful silence of the troop bay.

'Commander,' DuDeq said. The silence shattered. Allegra watched the chief's smile widen. The gunner was standing at the narrow observation port in the bay wall. Heaving the slummer girl's head up onto one shoulder and getting to her feet, she joined DuDeq by the port. Gohlandr moved up too.

Capricorn-Six was flying high above the chromatic sheen

of Undine's chemical seas, flanked by two gunships. Below, the commander and the two guardsmen could see a fleet of ocean-going vessels. There were fat troop carriers and medical freighters, escorted by sliver-hulled monitors and heavily-armed corvettes. Multi-hulled launch carriers bearing arc-platforms of Avenger Strike Fighters dominated the armada, trailing squat bomb vessels and torpedo boats in formation, while gunships and carriers ferried surviving personnel and materiel back to sleek gunboats and pocket frigates.

Lux Allegra slowly shook her head. Ordinarily such a gathering of local defence force and Undine Maritine vessels would have been an impressive sight. Allegra thought on the trap-jaw moon glowering down on them and the vanguard hordes of greenskin monsters they had faced at Hive Tyche. She thought on the alien swarm raining down on the ocean world and the billions she suspected were to come.

'It's not enough...' Lux Allegra murmured, the ghost of the smile fading from her lips. 'It's not nearly enough.'

FOUR

Incus Maximal – Hyboriax Cryoforge

Incus. Malleus. The hammer and the anvil.

The forge-worlds Incus Maximal and Malleus Mundi hung in the darkness of the void like a pair of pearls. Orbiting in synchronous rotation, the planets pirouetted each other and their distant star like spireball dancers. Their thousand-year performance came to an end, however, with the intervention of a third astral body. A planetary interloper. In the cryovolcanic haze between the two frozen worlds appeared a junker moon, the rusted plates and rivets of its impossibly armoured surface dusted with ice. The rogue body materialised between the binary forge-worlds, throwing the Adeptus Mechanicus planets into uncharacteristic chaos and disharmony.

The hololithic representation crackled and warped before fading. Moments later, the planets seared back to full resolution.

'Have the High Enginseer report to section nineteen and reroute power through the generatoria,' Altarius

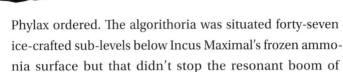

Phylax ordered. The algorithoria was situated forty-seven ice-crafted sub-levels below Incus Maximal's frozen ammonia surface but that didn't stop the resonant boom of detonations reverberating down through the structure.

Phylax processed the cold code-equivalent of incredulity. It was difficult to believe that the great ark ships of the Adeptus Mechanicus were shelling their own forge-world. His frost-bitten face might have still been his own, but the fibre bundles beneath were enhancements that required a moment to catch up with Phylax's rapid train of thought and occasional feeling.

In the ice-carved chamber adepts and servitors fussed about him, slipping the multi-limbed fusion of metal and flesh that was his body into his new robes: the hallowed red robes of the Fabricator Locum of Incus Maximal, a position Phylax had inherited a mere fourteen minutes and thirty-two seconds before. Fabricator Torqsi had been lost to the Mechanicus when Vostox Mons unexpectedly and explosively erupted, blowing its cryo-magma stack and accompanying forge complex clean off the face of the planet. Mistress Celestika had believed in meeting the xenos invasion head to head. She had led her temple tech-guard from the front, out onto the spotless plains of Freon-Astroika, at the head of two thousand deep-freeze adapted Kataphron battle-servitors fresh off the assembly lines. Warrior specimens of *Veridi giganticus* arrived on the ammonia flows in incalculable number, however, and the beast-forms had smashed Mistress Celestika and her Kataphron columns to smouldering scrap on the plain. Phylax's predecessor, Moritor Vulk, had simply locked himself away with a congressium of logi and calculus-engines while the alien invaders overwhelmed cryoforge after cryoforge across the ice world's surface. Concluding their statistical analysis of the invasion and associated factors, the congressium disbanded. Moritor then returned to his forge temple, disabled his aegis protocols and voluntarily uploaded a nano-infection that reduced the magnificence of his augmented form to rust and steaming spoilage. As next in runic line, the young but brilliant Magos Altarius Phylax became Fabricator Locum of Incus Maximal.

Servo-skulls and technodrones swarmed and swooped through the crackling hololithic display.

'Siege-Savant Entaurii,' Phylax addressed the Master of the Auxilia Myrmidon. 'Is it entirely necessary to have our own vessels execute an orbital bombardment right above our heads?'

'Entirely necessary, my lord,' Entaurii replied.

'That is the Hyboriax Forge Temple up there,' Phylax reminded him. 'The Mons Primus and planetary capital. It honours the Omnissiah as a technological wonder and it is bare-faced blasphemy to demolish it with our own guns.'

Borz Entaurii was a squat, heavily augmented soldier – more pneumatic piston than man. His hydraulics and barrel chest were encased in bronze plate and buried in broad, hooded robes that were dyed an Omnissiah-pleasing crimson. He was a veteran, blunt and lacking in imagination.

'Without the *Contrivenant* firing down on our position, my Lord Fabricator,' Entaurii said, 'there would be no position. The enemy xenos would already have breached our sub-levels.'

'Could the great ark's weaponry not find better purpose and employment in firing on the junker moon itself?' Phylax pressed.

'Both the *Aetnox* and the *Melanchola* were lost in such an experiment,' Entaurii said. 'The body's defences are too thick: armour, shielding and presumed moon rock beneath. Even the greatest of the Machine God's blessed weapons have failed to make an impression.'

'And what of our ground troops?' Phylax said.

A skitarii officer stepped forwards with his gas-masked head bowed. He was dressed in a mixture of ceremonial chainmail and white camouflage robes lined with fur. He had clearly seen recent action. Like Phylax himself, the skitarii officer's promotion had also been an impromptu necessity.

'Trib–' the soldier began, before correcting himself. 'Master Andromaq, of the Incunian Temple Praetoriax.'

'Master Andromaq,' Phylax acknowledged.

'My lord,' the master of skitarii said, 'even allowing for strategic models and assembly line reinforcement, our losses are grievous. Many of our armoured and Kataphron contingents were lost during first contact at Freon-Astroika. Skitarii of the Phaedrik Tenth Denticle, and the artillery batteries of the Ballisteria Algistra, have been decimated at Hoarzengrad and the Novolaris trenchworks are overrun.'

'Even the great war machine *Ordinatus Incus* lies in ruin on the Plain of Achromat,' Siege-Savant Entaurii added.

'Our numbers have been bolstered by the accelerated vat-production of gun-servitors,' Master Andromaq admitted, 'but the genetors are unhappy with the results. The demands of an expedited process have created a higher rate of failures and abominates. Beyond that, the munitiomats are barely configured and the enhanced infantry is fresh off the surgical slab.'

'But we have veteran temple guard...'

'The mainstay of our forces were garrisoned at each of the regional Mons-capitals,' Master Andromaq told him. 'Many of the forge temples crowning the cryovolcanoes were destroyed in the eruptions.'

'Estimated operational capacity?' the Fabricator Locum asked.

'Twenty-two point six seven per cent,' Andromaq said. 'Estimated.'

'With such a force, Master Andromaq, can you conceive of a defensive strategy or tactical advantage that might meet the demands of these extraordinary events?'

'No, Fabricator Locum,' Andromaq replied simply. 'Complex tactics can be met with complex tactics. They create options. The *Veridi giganticus* restrict our responses with strategic simplicity. There are just more of them. Beyond a certain magnitude, the numbers will not be worked or contrived. In my opinion, we are beyond that point.'

'Estimated planetary casualties?' Phylax asked.

'Eighty million,' Phylax's spindly high logist informed him, scuttling forwards. As calculus-principal of the congressium, he was best placed to make such an astronomical estimate. 'And rising, Lord Fabricator.'

'Has the congressium revised its statistical appraisal?' Phylax queried.

'Only downwards, my lord,' the high logist replied. 'As the

full magnitude of the xenos invasion has been revealed to us, we have collated data and updated our recommendations. We submit for your consideration a revised estimation of zero point four per cent chance of victory.'

'You are saying that we cannot repel this invasion.'

'We're saying that the Machine God's servants on Incus Maximal cannot survive this invasion, my lord.'

Altarius Phylax allowed himself a moment to process what his high logist was saying.

'And of our sister forge-world?'

'By the vast majority of comparative measures, data from Malleus Mundi tells us they are faring worse than we are,' the high logist informed him.

'Siege-savant?'

'They have the Legio Fornax,' Borz Entaurii said. 'And what I wouldn't give for their god-machines right now on our hallowed ice.'

'Ambassador Utherica,' Phylax called.

'Lord Fabricator?' a silver-skinned crone in dark robes said as she presented herself before him. Her aged face was overlaid with circuitry that glittered with tiny synaptic sparks.

'Do we have word or cant from the Lady of the Furnace?' Phylax asked the ambassador from Malleus Mundi.

The crone cackled code back at him before drifting absently into Gothic. 'Only that she would have you know that the Titans of the Legio Fornax bring down the vengeance of the Omnissiah on the xenos vermin and, Machine God willing, shall burn them from the glacial surface of our world.'

'I don't mean to contradict the Ambassador...' Savant Entaurii began.

'Proceed,' Phylax invited. The hololith magnified the Malleus Mundi forge-world. Even from orbit, the planetary damage was obvious and catastrophic. One-half of the planet had been torn up and reduced to berg-scattered slush. Mons temples and cryoforge clusters streamed black destruction and the glittering white surface of the ice world was clouded with the black murk of alien hordes, swallowing the world like a growing shadow.

'They're troop movements,' Phylax said, understanding immediately what the siege-savant was attempting to communicate.

'Yes, my lord.'

'I suspect,' the Fabricator Locum said, 'that our own world appears similarly from orbit.'

'I can bring up the...'

'That won't be necessary,' Phylax told Entaurii.

Altarius Phylax tried to reach out beyond the cold logic of his directives and protocols. This was not without difficulty, and felt vague and unnatural. Feel he did, however, and he found his way to a part of his humanity all but forgotten – the part that ached without reason for those lost to him and those he was losing. He allowed fancies and visualisations to sear sharply to focus in his mind. He dwelled on the dead – their corpses hacked to meat and wiring on the ice. He hurt for the living, those blankly processing their last orders and impulses under the barbarian invaders' blades. He experienced a connection – something that didn't require cant or code but travelled broad and far. A connection not only between himself and all Incusians, but also between the billion victims of the twin forge-worlds.

The feeling was incredible and unpleasant. He indulged its overwhelming power a moment more before allowing the prejudice of his protocols their former supremacy.

'Ambassador – Legio Fornax or not, I think that the Lady of the Furnace has to accept her forge-world is lost,' Phylax said finally. The crone said nothing. The attendant magi and forge masters stiffened. 'As must I.'

'What do you mean, Lord Fabricator?' the high logist asked.

'I mean, it is time to let Incus Maximal go.'

'The Lords Diagnostica will not sanction such an action,' the high logist informed Phylax with cautious force. 'They will speak against it at the machine altars. They will claim Incus Maximal as the Omnissiah's sovereign territory and the Machine God's subjects as the ordained defenders of such rites – to the last man and machine.'

'This is not a cult matter,' Phylax said simply. 'Besides – as Fabricator Locum do I not speak for the Omnissiah on Incus Maximal?'

'Yes, my lord.'

'Then it is decided. If I don't act now – right now – there won't be anyone left at the machine altars to preach to,' Altarius Phylax said. He looked to Ambassador Utherica. 'Perhaps our action might stir the Lady of the Furnace to similar mercies and to defy the will of her own Diagnosticians.'

'You speak of mercy, my lord, a most illogical–' the high logist began.

'I speak of sense,' Phylax interrupted, 'common and good. A most Omnissian virtue, I assure you. The enemy have invaded. The enemy has succeeded. The Machine God does not demand the lives of all in order for such a precept to be accepted. Savant Entaurii?'

'Yes, Lord Fabricator.'

'I mean to evacuate all remaining Incusians from the forge-world surface. The Lords Diagnostica will be charged with the preservation of the machine altars and the transfer of technodivinity and knowledge contained within. The high logist and the congressium will begin ratiocinatia and matrices for a successful off-world evacuation of all surviving tech-priests, menials and technologies and constructs that can be transferred. Materiel is to remain. Skitarii forces are to disable or destroy what cannot be moved, upon withdrawal.'

'Is that not blasphemy, my lord?' Master Andromaq put to Phylax.

'It would be blasphemy to allow the Machine God's holy instruments and the spirits within to be scrapped and corrupted to alien purpose,' the Fabricator Locum insisted. 'I expect you to communicate such reality to your forces, Master Andromaq. It will lend them certainty and help them through their conflicting protocols.'

'And from me, my lord?' Entaurii asked.

'A planetary exodus point, siege-savant,' Phylax said. 'A holdpoint through which to funnel fleeing forge-worlders.'

Entaurii nodded: 'There is an auxiliary spaceport near the northern pole: the Lambdagard. It's a freight station – largely automated – that is principally used for the storage and exportation of scrap and toxic materials.'

'But the temperatures...' Master Andromaq began.

'The polar conditions will be a challenge even for native

Incusians,' Entaurii admitted, 'but similarly so for the alien invader. The region has the smallest concentration of enemy forces on the planet.'

'It sounds serviceable,' the Fabricator Locum said. 'Depots and storage terminals for waiting evacuees. Ice-strips for ferrying transports.'

'But the deep cold, my lord,' Andromaq pressed. 'Think of the losses.'

'They will be less than if we evacuate survivors through the xenos hordes,' Phylax said. 'I'd rather our people took their chances with their home world than with the enemy.'

'Yes, Lord Fabricator.'

'Siege-savant,' Phylax ordered, looking to Entaurii. 'You must now fight a rearguard action. You must order the Ark vessels *Contrivenant*, *Archmagi Alpharatz* and *The Weakness of Flesh* to risk low orbit and receive as many forge-worlders as they can from the pole. Find hump shuttles, freightskiffs, lighters: anything that can carry survivors. They must keep evacuating survivors from the Lambdagard for as long as they can. The congressium will consider how best to communicate our intentions to defending forces and the forge-world populace.'

'What if the invaders hit the Ark ships?' the high logist posited. Entaurii shook his head.

'So far the aliens' tactics have not run to anything approaching such complexity,' the siege-savant informed him. 'They want the planet. They want it by force.'

'Three vessels will not be enough for your survivors,' Ambassador Utherica piped up, morose and subdued.

'And what would you suggest, ambassador?' Phylax

challenged. 'I hope to the Machine God you're right. I hope that the invader leaves that many forge-worlders alive.'

'Use my diplomatic protocols,' Utherica offered. 'They carry the authority of an Archmagos or Collegia Imperatrix. Use them to order the factory ships, the frigate *Ratchet* and the Titanica temple supertransport *Deus Charios* off station above Malleus Mundi to participate in the evacuation.'

'Ambassador, the Lady of the Furnace may still need those vessels,' Phylax protested.

'She will not,' Utherica insisted. 'The Lady will die on her forge-world, with her people. Her Diagnostica priests will not allow anything else. They lack your flesh-wisdom, Lord Phylax.'

Altarius Phylax nodded his appreciation.

'We shall honour the Lady's sacrifice,' he told the ambassador, 'and if I live to see the day, I will personally lead the effort to take her forge-world back from the xenos along with my own.'

The ambassador bowed her aged features and handed Borz Entaurii her protocols.

'Where shall we go?' the high logist asked.

'Corewards,' Altarius Phylax said. 'We shall join forces with our brother priests on the forge-worlds of the inner segmentum.'

'And if we experience failure there?' the high logist pushed him.

'Then, Omnissiah willing, to the forge-world principal,' the Fabricator Locum told him grimly, 'where we shall fight on the holy red earth of Mars itself. Pray to the Machine God that it does not come to that.'

FIVE

Eidolica – Alcazar Astra

'Switch to infrared, brothers,' Second Captain Maximus Thane ordered. With Chapter Master Alameda lost to the first enemy wave and First Captain Garthas coordinating defences from the tactical oratorium, Thane was the ranking Fists Exemplar officer on the bastion. As his auto-senses responded and a thermal filter dropped across his optics, the absolute darkness of the Eidolican night was transformed. Instead of the freezing blackness of the desert, Thane could spectro-differentiate the deeper blues of the dune horizon and the starless void above. The captain knew that distant stellar pinpricks were lost to the ugly irregularity of the attack moon hovering directly overhead. Cast in total ecliptic shadow by the Space Marine home world, the only evidence that the monstrous planetoid was there were the descent streaks of xenos-infested meteorites and thunderbolting assault boats.

That was, until the first wave of attacks.

Red dots of alien fervour appeared on the contrast line of

the horizon. Isolated heat signatures marking the storming advance of vanguard hulks soon became a polychromatic nightmare that swallowed the false-colour cobalt of the desert. Even Thane and his Space Marine brothers – accustomed to the grandeur of the galaxy and a life of war – were surprised at the sheer number of invaders. The night desert was awash with xenos foebreeds: a deluge of enemy targets that confounded auspex and targeters with their swarming magnitude.

The Adeptus Astartes on the ramparts stood in stoic silence as the enemy rampaged across the Akbar promethium fields. The orks smashed through radiance harvesters and enclosures of photovoltaic cells. They thundered through township after township, flattening worksteads, generatoria and battery silos before destroying the promethium wells. Through their optics, the Space Marines watched columns of white flame jet into the dark skies. The towers of fiery fury and the saturation of the sand with the drizzle of crude promethium did little to slow the alien monsters.

The captain heard the clunk of armoured boots on the hull plating behind him and turned to see Mendel Reoch, Apothecary of the Second Company. On the blasted hull of the star fort and amongst the scorched ceramite of his brothers, the white paint of the Apothecary's plate advertised itself like a dare to the enemy. Unlike the captain, the Apothecary had braved the Eidolican night without his helmet. What was left of a ruined mouth and jaw had long been fused into the ugly grille of a half-helm. A pair of bionoptics peered over the grille, glowing darkly like a pair of colour-tinted spectacles.

'Won't the chief need you in the Apothecarion?' Thane asked his old friend.

'If the Emperor's work is accomplished out here,' Reoch grizzled back through the vox-modulated grille, 'then I shan't be needed anywhere. Wouldn't that be a treat?'

'Not afraid of a little real work, are you, Apothecary?' Thane teased grimly.

Reoch drew his bolt pistol and looked down its sights at the deck.

'There are labours,' the Apothecary replied, 'and there are labours of love. If you're asking if I'd rather be in the Apothecarion sewing our brothers back together or taking the enemy apart out here, I shouldn't have to answer you that.'

'Both your knowledge and skill are welcome here, brother,' Thane told him honestly. 'Our guests, less so.'

Reoch looked up from his pistol. The glow of his implant optics intensified as he seemed to see for the first time the advancing tide of targets washing up against the void bastion. The Apothecary grunted, as though disgusted at the inconvenience.

'Don't be discourteous now, brother,' Reoch returned. 'They'll get the same welcome as any other species trespassing within the borders of the Emperor's Holy Imperium: they'll be shot.'

A small cluster of Apothecarion serfs had followed their master out onto the bastion in their plain white robes. Reoch handed the lead servant the weighty pistol. 'These sights need realigning,' the Apothecary told him. 'See to it, and this time do it properly. These damned creatures could have done a better job. Have no less respect for the

instruments that take life in the field than those that preserve it on the apothecarion slab. I pray for your sake that you have brought my reserve.'

Another serf handed his master a second bolt pistol. Reoch fell to examining the reserve instrument before telling the servants: 'Well, it will have to do, won't it? It's not as though the enemy will wait the time it will take you to perfect your duties. I will devise your corrections later – if I am alive to do so.'

'Will you be needing us, Master Reoch?' one of the serfs mustered the courage to ask. Beneath their hoods the servants had all been watching the darkness and listening to the cacophony of the monsters beyond.

'No,' the Apothecary told him harshly. 'Only the Emperor's Finest are required here. Report to the Chief Apothecary. Perhaps he can find you a mop and bucket for the blood. Now get out of my sight.'

The serfs headed back towards the launch bays, leaving a weapon rack behind. The rack was laden with reserve magazines of bolt ammunition, simple gladius blades and the serrated length of the Apothecary's chainsword. The mirrored finish of the weapon gleamed with clinical lethality. Reoch scooped the white dome of his half-helm from the rack and pulled it down over his bionics and scarred face-flesh. The half-helm gave a hydraulic sigh as it locked into place with the grille of its counterpart section.

Captain Thane had had Brother Aquino request of the signum-tower array any reports of intercepted communications between enemy contingents or ground-hordes and the attack moon. There was naught forthcoming. The captain found this unsettling. Falling to the surface of Eidolica in brute clutches, descent survivors amassed in murderous throngs – before, like blood coagulating in the veins and organs of a corpse, throngs became mobs and mobs became clan swarms. The barbarians seemed to be guided by a common brutality or unthinking brotherhood. Without the aid of conventional communications, beasts that ordinarily would prey on one another with claw, fang and mongrel weaponry found each other across the black sands of Eidolica. They were drawn down on the Adeptus Astartes' position, guided by some predacious, gestalt impulse.

Thane considered that it might simply be lack of resistance that was driving the creatures on towards them with such speed. Fortunately, the Akbar promethium fields were all but deserted during the season of the Noxtide. Hardy caravans of nomadic workers and their families had migrated east to the Sheldrahc and Pharad fields, leaving automated jack-wells and photovoltaic harvesters under the seasonal supervision of crisp-skinned servitors in stone bubble-bunkers. Thane could only imagine what havoc the enemy were wreaking there or further east in the Great Basin and Tharkis Flats, where it was the time of the Yielding and Terra's tithe was due.

That was Seventh Captain Dentor's problem, although vox-chatter seemed to indicate that things were not going well. In the desert darkness, cursed with an exposed position, defending hundreds of thousands of nomad-civilians and supported by an ill-equipped promethium fields militia, Dentor and his company-brothers were at the heart of a swiftly-unfolding slaughter.

The auspectoria confirmed, however, that of the invader forces raining to the Eidolican sands from the attack moon, the vast majority had converged on the *Alcazar Astra* – the fortress-monastery of the Fists Exemplar Space Marine Chapter. Post-formation, the Fists Exemplar had been assigned to watch over the Rubicante Flux, a warp storm that plagued the Abra Sector. Manifesting in Imperial space on the outskirts of the Segmentum Solar and uncomfortably close to Ancient Terra, the Rubicante Flux was sporadic in its eruptions, visiting occasional space hulks, mutant incursions and renegade Space Marine hosts on the surrounding systems. The newly formed Fists Exemplar Chapter was given responsibility for garrisoning the storm-wracked region of wilderness space afflicted by the rapidly appearing and disappearing Flux. For this duty, they were equipped with the *Alcazar Astra*: a heavily-armed star fortress that had done good service for the Fists Exemplar's parent Legion, the Imperial Fists, in the Volgotha Deeps during the dark days of the Heresy. Chapter Chaplains maintained that the star fort was a gift from Rogal Dorn himself.

That had been until the Rubicante Flux's most recent encroachment. Although the eruption lasted mere hours, the rift event was colossal in magnitude – wrecking subsector shipping, disrupting communications and heralding the inception of numerous doomsday cults across the Imperial worlds of the region. The eruption's most ambitious victim, though, was the *Alcazar Astra* itself. At the time the star fort was being transported through the neighbouring Frankenthal System by Chapter tow-tenders and monitors, only to be blown off course and into the gravitational embrace of Frankenthal's star by the storm shock wave. Through the skill of Chapter Master Dantalion and his castellan-commanders, the *Alcazar Astra* was guided towards the star's nearest planet and beached in the black sands of Eidolica. Grounded, the fort was forever without hope of feeling again the cold kiss of the void on its armour plating. Three of its four ancient engine-columns had been destroyed in the impact. The secrets of the plasma-drives' construction had been lost to the weaponsmiths and Tech-marines of the Chapter, and so the beached star fort had become a planetary fortress.

All Fists Exemplar Space Marines gave thanks for that day and for their first Chapter Master. Oriax Dantalion had survived the Heresy but had lost his life in the fortress-monastery's crash landing. Many Space Marines of the Fists Exemplar Chapter believed themselves and their gene-seed saved that day for some greater purpose, perhaps involving the vagaries of the Rubicante Flux.

Standing atop the ramparts of the fortress-monastery – the shattered superstructure of the *Alcazar Astra* half buried in black sand, its mighty baroque architecture and cathe-dral towers askew but still reaching for the void – Captain Maximus Thane awaited his enemy. As the monsters roared their way through the darkness, the captain's heat vision clouded with colour. As they got closer, the hulking crea-tures seared red, their hot rage edging up the brute length of their cool-blue weaponry.

Thane felt the *clunk* of priming mechanisms through the armour plating beneath his boots.

'That's more like it,' Apothecary Reoch observed.

Machine-spirits were stirring. Ammunition was being autoloaded. The mighty defence lasers of the star fort were pointed uselessly at the open sky, their wrath already directed with futility at the pockmarked darkness of the attack moon's surface. Upon becoming a grounded fortification, the Fists Exemplar had worked hard to adapt the *Alcazar Astra* for a possible land assault. From the tactical oratorium, First Captain Garthas had ordered the mounted gatling blasters and mega-bolters cleared for action. Over the vox-channel, Thane heard Eighth Captain Xontague report targets on Transept South, followed swiftly by Fifth Captain Tyrian on Transept East. As both Ninth Captain Hieronimax and Kastril, the Scout Company captain, simultaneously called in enemy signatures from Fortress-Monastery North, it became obvious that the alien barbarians were to employ tactics no more ambitious than overwhelming the Fists Exemplar from all sides simultaneously. Thane felt combined respect and hatred for his enemy rise up the back of his throat like bile. With their sheer numbers, the xenos invader could afford such a wasteful strategy. It could and probably would work for them. Thane promised himself that he would make the mindless foe pay for their thuggish overconfidence.

The captain turned to Brother Aquino. Ordinarily the Fists Exemplar Space Marines left their armour unpainted. It was Chapter tradition and requirement, although the conditions on Eidolica swiftly gave the ceramite plate a sooty, chromatic sheen, the same bronzed quality possessed by the nozzles and muzzle-guards of company flamers and meltaguns. Through the captain's infrared filters, Aquino's armour appeared dark blue, his company banner a ghostly trapezium cut out of the sky. Thane nodded to the grim, aged standard bearer, prompting him to call in their own sightings.

Sergeant Hoque approached along the void rampart. The infrared outline of the veteran's armour was rent and battle-beaten from an earlier reconnaissance out on the rocky dunes. Hoque moved from Space Marine to Space Marine, personally lending his affirmation or disapproval of positioning, stance and weapon readiness. With fraternal love and opprobrium, the sergeant smacked helms with his gauntlet and pointed out beyond the barrels of boltguns with ceramite fingers.

Across the vox-channel, Thane heard Techmarines offer litanies of forward assistance and shell clearance before First Captain Garthas gave the order to open fire. The crenellated nests, gargoyles and statues into which the mega-bolters and gatling blasters were built shuddered to the rhythmic cacophony. The weapons' fire crashed about the false-colour shapes of Sergeant Hoque and the Space Marines of the Second Company, their gaping barrels wands of hot brilliance through the infrared filters.

Captain Thane stared out across the dark sands. Scarlet silhouettes, jagged and ungainly, formed a closing wall of hulking forms. Spikes and serrations decorated the muscular giants, while the shapes of brute-bore barrels, monstrous hackers and mechanical claws promised butchery to come. Thane felt the exhilaration of the gunfire reverberate through his being, and he watched with no little satisfaction as mega-bolter shells ripped through

the oncoming foe, tearing the monstrosities to hot shreds of flesh and turning the barbarian front lines into clouds of red mist. Line after line of the monstrosities fell as the autofire reached deeper into the enemy ranks.

And then, one by one, he felt the guns about him thunder to emptiness. Almost immediately the routine of reloading began but in the calmness that followed, with the chatter of the guns still carried distantly on the breeze, Thane had opportunity to witness the xenos recovery. Holes in the vanguard closed rapidly, with beasts almost crawling over each other to be at the forefront of the slaughter. They stamped through the demolished carcasses of their fallen and howled their alien derision and delight. Within seconds, the impact of the barrage was imperceptible.

'Well, isn't that a thing,' Reoch said.

'Are you seeing this?' Maximus Thane voxed through to the tactical oratorium.

'I am,' First Captain Garthas responded grimly. Thane heard him speak to an oratorium officer. 'Launch the gunships.'

As the mega-bolters and gatling blasters resumed the futility of defensive fire protocols, Thane's plate registered the heatwash of afterburners as Thunderhawks and Storm Eagle gunships blasted from the unsealing launch bays behind them. As the craft screamed their fury above, Brother Aquino's banner thrashed and twirled. Thane watched the Fists Exemplar craft blaze away, the cool blue of their armoured hull plating bright against the deeper blue-black of the Eidolican skies. Only their triple engines glowed searing white and left a chromatic scale in the trail of their afterburners.

The formations streaked away: bomb-laden Thunderhawks flanked by lower, strafing Storm Eagle gunships. The screaming spectacle was met with celebratory gunfire from the savages. They couldn't see the aircraft, but they could hear them. Unleashing their brute weaponry at the heavens, the beasts raged at the approaching thunder. They were rewarded with swooping passes from the Storm Eagles, who cut through the bestial throngs with vapour blasts from their prow multi-meltas and thick beams of searing light from wing-mounted lascannons. As the gunships weaved and strafed clear, the Thunderhawk formations dropped their incendiary bomb payloads. The desert-world night seared with blinding explosions that turned swarms of monstrous xenos into fields of death.

While even the most sizeable monsters were vaporised at the heart of the detonations, many thousands of surrounding beasts were set alight. This was exacerbated by the promethium that had drizzled over everything from the ruptured wells. Soon the dark desert sands were a dance of blinding colour and it was difficult to make out the enemy from the inferno that had engulfed them.

Switching from infrared back to regular spectra, Maximus Thane saw the midnight dunes lit up in a sea of flame. Against another enemy such a devastating strategy would have been a game changer. There were few species that were not susceptible to violent changes in temperature. Most forms of flesh in the galaxy burned in the fires of battle, and ork flesh should have been no different. But as Thane watched the beasts storm towards him, illuminated by the flames snaking about their scraps of armour and brute forms, it seemed to make little difference.

Apart from in size, the greenskins didn't seem any different in physiology than other savage clanbreeds the captain had fought. Perhaps it was size alone that made the difference, Thane mused. As great, hulking monsters sculpted from leathery skin, gnarled bone and muscle, the Fists Exemplar captain reasoned that perhaps there was less need than usual in this sub-species for a complex nervous system and a brain that could interpret the intense agonies of being burned alive.

Stampeding through the flames, the enemy charged on. Fear didn't slow their advance. Pain didn't show on their snaggle-tusk faces. Death was an end beyond the simple imaginings of such creatures. They swarmed and they stormed the *Alcazar Astra*. The desert roared with flame. Alien war cries filled the air. The void bastion crashed with the fire of gatling blasters. Among the pure havoc of battle, with the fortress-monastery's crooked spires reaching up beyond the ring of fire and the sea of thundering green flesh beyond, Second Captain Maximus Thane and his Fists Exemplar stood as calm, still and impassive as the decorative gargoyles about them. The statues would do little to ward off the evil approaching the *Alcazar Astra* today.

'You've studied xenos physiology. Any advice?' Thane put to his friend. 'I'm opening a channel.'

The Apothecary angled his bone-white helmet to one side. 'If you must,' Reoch replied with little appetite for the duty.

'Second Company,' Thane called across an open vox-channel, 'stand by for the Apothecary's observations.'

'On average,' Reoch broadcast, 'the enemy appears larger than the feral specimens we exterminated on Borksworld. Those on Konrax were mere runts to these monsters.'

'And?' the captain asked as Reoch's enthusiasm for the task trailed off further.

'Their ability to soak up the impact of our weaponry will be considerable,' Reoch warned. 'Still, I doubt the increased thickness of a larger skull will resist the blessed path of our bolt-rounds.'

'So headshots are the order of the day,' Maximus Thane agreed.

'And night,' the Apothecary mused, looking up into the deep sky.

'And at close quarters?' Thane pushed.

'A larger biped opponent presents vulnerabilities at the throat and abdomen,' Reoch told Second Company. 'But don't bother with the loins. Go for the legs. Dismembered specimens brought down to the sand will present a much greater range of kill-sites and vulnerabilities. This is all I have,' the Apothecary signed off.

Thane gave Reoch the blank glare of his faceplate and closed the channel. The Apothecary stared back.

'They're your men,' Reoch stated, allowing his optics to burn beyond his friend, through Sergeant Hoque and his defence formations and out across the green savagery that rolled on towards them like a furious formation of agri-world rotary threshers. 'Talk to them... while you still can.'

Thane's head fell to a solemn nod. He looked to Sergeant Hoque. Behind the veteran, the flame-swathed hulks stomped on towards the Fists Exemplar. Uncouth weapons – hacked, torched and sharpened from heavy-metal scrap and hull plating – came up like a jagged forest of death. Brute gunnery, barrels gaping wide, chugged lead at the *Alcazar Astra*. Elated weapons fire, wild and pathetically out of range, had afflicted the sand and sky for some time. The monsters could barely contain their exultant ferocity on the final, teeming approach, however, and metal slugs sang off the star fort's void plating in an aimless barrage. In the shell storm, occasional ordnance found its mark amongst the cover-blessed Fists Exemplar. For the most part, the jubilant boom of greenskin weaponry at rapidly closing range was simply an ear-splitting distraction.

'The company is cleared to load, sergeant,' Thane said.

'Second Company, ready weapons!' Hoque reiterated across the open channel. Fists Exemplar Space Marines took sickle magazines from where they hung mag-locked to their belts and loaded their Umbra-pattern boltguns.

'Maximus,' Mendel Reoch said, with an unusual, modulated softness. 'Talk to them.'

Maximus Thane allowed his mind to drift back to Charnassica. To that first day, stepping off the Thunderhawk ramp and into the blood-slick earth of conquest. He remembered his young body, the power and possibilities it offered. He relived the rawness of his black carapace and the sting of his interface plugs. He ached with the presence of the Emperor in his hearts, the nearness of the enemy, the imminence of his first kill, the cold beauty of battle into which he had been dropped. He had been a full brother of the Fists Exemplar mere days, yet there he was – a living, breathing instrument of the Emperor's will. He had everything he needed to prosecute that will on the battle lines of Charnassica, yet what would he have given for the warmth of words in the darkness of his helmet at that moment – words freely given in the fortification of the soul.

'Second Company, this is your captain,' Thane said into his helmet vox-feed. As he spoke, the invader monstrosities closed, growing in apparent size and ferocity. 'We face a dangerous foe. Warlords unreasoning stand at the head of an enemy innumerable. Doubt not the threat they present. Take no comfort in past experience with the green plague. These monsters are a beast-host we have never faced, wielding technologies undreamt of.'

The thunder of alien footfalls struck the void plating, where the fallen fortress-monastery of the Fists Exemplar met the blacks sands of Eidolica.

'Trust in your commanders. Trust in your training. Trust in the plate on your back and the weapons in your gauntlets. Trust in the noble history of your Legion and the legacy of your primarch, knowing that it is through his wisdom that you stand here today: a brotherhood, a Chapter, exemplars of your kind. Know that I am with you. Know that First Captain Garthas is with you. Know that the spirits of Chapter Master Alameda and Chapter Master Dantalion – the chosen of Dorn – fight at your side.'

The beast hordes entered optimum range. The killzone beckoned. Thane felt his men lean into their boltguns. He felt them pick out their first targets. He felt the singular will of one hundred superhumans: their unbreakable faith, the pride in their purpose, their sharp hatred of the xenos.

'Most of all, know that it is the Emperor's blood that flows through your veins and He will not let you fail. Eidolica is His. It is Imperial sand and dirt. It isn't much, but it belongs to humanity and as such it is not the Fists Exemplars' to give away. I know you will do your best. I know you will make your Chapter and your Emperor proud. Give all you have in His name, as He has given for you. Bring all your genetic gifts, your talents and abilities, to bear. Live through your plate. Be one with your weapons. Fulfil, my battle-brothers, the purpose for which you were ultimately created.'

In one fluid movement, Thane slammed a sickle mag home into the breech of his own Umbra-pattern boltgun. The Umbra was a venerable pattern, thought of as uncouth and archaic after the necessities of the Heresy. Despite lacking the finesse and refinements of other patterns, Thane found the Umbra to be a reliable and reassuringly bombastic bolter. A Chapter workhorse of a weapon.

'This is Maximus Thane, captain of the Second Company, Fists Exemplar Chapter. The order is given...'

Thane leaned into the boltgun and picked out the first of the unfortunate green beasts to die: a pale monstrosity, brutally etched with scars and jangling with rings, tribal trinkets and piercings.

'Fire.'

SIX

Terra – the Imperial Palace

On the Feast Day of Deliverance, it was traditional for the Senatorum Imperialis to restrict its meetings to the Imperium's most urgent business. The Imperial Palace was lifted by evensong; blessed incense was burned by the brazier and both Adeptus Custodes and Astartes attendants were required to adopt ceremonial attire. The cavernous halls and corridors of the Palace were decked with reverential tapestries and flocks of winged cherubim read from endless scrolls the lists of fallen notables and petitionaries. Prayers and benedictions were offered and armies of planetary ambassadors admitted in rotating attendances to witness ritual silences, followed by volley shots and a salute issued by honour guards of decorated Lucifer Blacks.

Beyond the urgent business of their own mighty bureaucracies, the High Lords of Terra were occasionally called to order during the solemnities and celebrations. The Samarkan hive plague had necessitated such measures, as had the mutiny at Zyracuse. Since the Ardamantuan Atrocity,

the tedium of unscheduled council meetings had become a common distraction for the Senatorum Imperialis.

Today's urgent business regarded the loss of the shrine worlds of the Jeronimus Fyodora cluster and that glittering jewel of piety, the cardinal world of Fleur-de-Fides. Most days there were reports of some kind of distant disaster. It had become almost commonplace. Such news – if reported publically – would have thrown Terra's billions into a state of panic and mobilised thousands of interest groups and influentials.

It was agreed that this was not in the best interests of the Imperium. Instead the horror of such catastrophes was restricted to the staid and stuffy assemblages of the High Lords: informal meetings of the Twelve in which the great and good of Terra put such tragedies in context.

'A great tragedy... indeed.'

'I believe my confessor attended the college-cathedra at Fleur-de-Fides.'

'A beautiful world: a real loss to the Imperium.'

'Cardinal Creutzfeldt will be looking for another seat, I suppose.'

'Isn't Gilbersia part of the Fyodora Cluster? No, wait. I'm thinking of the Outer Trinities.'

'Dreadful business...'

Loss of life, calculated by the billion, put unnecessary strain on the mind of the common Imperial citizen. The destruction of worlds, sometimes a score at a time, stoked patriotic notions of galacticism – and the suspicion that humanity was losing its grip of its precious empire among the stars.

The twelve men and women gathered in the Anesidoran

Chapel did not deal in such sentimentalities. They were perpetually lost in a blizzard of decisions, quantifications and bureaucracy in which the considerations of bounty and starvation, war and peace, life and death, were measured by planet, by subsector and segmentum. In a galactic game with an unimaginable number of pieces in play, it wasn't difficult for even the greatest minds and keenest ambitions of the Senatorum to become desensitised to the importance of individual details. Indeed, over time, even the most experienced of players tended to become blind to the board for the profusion of pieces. Within a parliament of such minds, even minor problems become exacerbated. In the kingdom of the deaf, dumb and blind, problems with small beginnings – small, at least, on a galactic scale – had a way of gathering irresistible momentum.

From their own legions of aides and overseers, the great Lords of Terra would have fragments of the same story. Some might have glimpsed certain characters amongst a greater cast; some a significant twist of the plot or timely reveal, nonsensical without knowledge of the events leading up to it; some might even have a narrative of doom laid before them but not know it. A tale with all the important words removed, a cloze exercise in fate... a puzzle of the calamity to come. What none of them had was the most essential feature of the story – the end.

Juskina Tull had colluded with her chartist captains to raise the price of passage and transportation between the segmentum core and the rimward sectors, but had not foreseen the decimation of her freighter fleets and the severance of ancient trade routes.

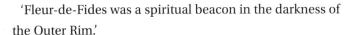

'Fleur-de-Fides was a spiritual beacon in the darkness of the Outer Rim.'

'To be sure.'

The Martian Kubik, Fabricator General and vox-piece for the Cult Mechanicus, had his own empire to look to. Can a man, even an augmeticised transhuman, serve two masters and serve them both equally? Kubik seemed to spend most of his time aboard his consular barge moving between Ancient Terra and the Red Planet, but in the cold corridors of his mechanical heart, Kubik answered only to the Omnissiah. During the Great Heresy, the two planets had been at war. The Heresy was long over and a cult confederacy – as strong as it was uneasy – had been re-established. As Fabricator General, it was Kubik's faithful duty to serve the logic of the Machine God. Today, that logic dictated an alliance of mutual benefit. It did not preclude the action of respectful partners in their own interest. Never again would mighty Mars serve as the battered barbican to Fortress Terra. Kubik would see the Red Planet protected and its empire remain strong and ruthlessly efficient.

It was because of this that the Fabricator General had been made aware of the gateway threat of the xenos Chromes. Ruthless efficiency had secretly fed the Inquisition the selected data required to justify a Critical Situation Packet – despite the fact that Kubik himself then had to denounce its credibility for political advantage. Ruthless efficiency had placed the gifted magos Phaeton Laurentis with the Imperial Fists on Ardamantua, after the bombastic Chapter Master Cassus Mirhen predictably took up the cause. Ruthless efficiency would see the Mechanicus through a disaster that Kubik's legion of logisticians had told him was inevitable. Ruthless efficiency would ensure that only the Machine God's servants had the very best quality data and that the Martian empire would survive the coming storm.

'Fleur-de-Fides was second only to Serenitrix in its global devotions.'

'Is seat Serenitrix open?'

'Serenitrix would be a good fit for Cardinal Creutzfeldt.'

Kubik exchanged programmed pleasantries with the freakish Sark and Anwar. Volquan Sark and Abdulias Anwar – Masters of the Astronomican and Adeptus Astra Telepathica respectively – were among the Imperium's most powerful psykers. They were all but beings of a different plane. With Helad Gibran, Paternoval Envoy of the Navigator Families, they had helped weave the intricate web of immaterial translation routes and astrotelepathic conduits that overlaid the Imperium corporeal. Without their empyreal dominion and supporting networks, the Imperium would grind to a halt like a rust-fused piece of ancient machinery. If they hadn't been so invested in seeking greater representation and influence for their mutant interests, they might have come to comprehend the ragged holes in their gossamer meshwork. They might have seen the speed at which the delicate fabric of the Imperium would unravel with the slaughter of their psychic servants across the rimward sectors. They might have understood the unscheduled disruption suffered by their dour League of Black Ships and the voracious hunger of an Astronomican-sustaining Emperor.

The Grand Provost Marshal looked on. Vernor Zeck was a hulk of a man, although half of his bulk was made up by augmetic prosthetics. His skin grafting and bionics were evidence of a lifetime spent working city-hives of inequity on Macromunda and working up through the ranks of the Adeptus Arbites – enforcing, hunting and judging corruption in the hearts of lesser men. His square jaw betrayed disinterest, whatever he forced his eyes to suggest, and in doing so Zeck revealed the very nature of his calling. The Provost Marshal could track a consignment of narcotics up through the hive, down to its very last grain. He could beat confessions from mutants, spire nobles and even fellow arbitrators in precinct house dungeons. He could preside over courts for months, sometimes years at a time, passing judgement on sector-spanning criminal enterprises so involved and complex that they would burn out a calculus-logi's cogitator. But among the ancients of the Senatorum, blinded by tedium of the most intense kind, Zeck found that his nose for criminality and corruption abandoned him. The occasional sniffs of malfeasance – suspected abuses, secrets of self-interest, profiteering – were ignored by the Grand Provost Marshal. Like a cyber-mastiff before a river or a sewer-channel of effluent, Zeck lost the scent, his suspicions carried off by a stream of banal bureaucracy.

'Perhaps a donation of some kind would be in order.'

'For the greater palatial families.'

'For the palatials, yes.'

The Lord Commander and Ekharth, the Master of the Administratum, were guiltier than most of inaction. If the Imperium were a ship, buffeted in a sea of circumstance, at the mercy of galactic chance, then information was its anchor. With an Imperium of information at their augmented fingertips, or at the fingertips of a chancellor, archivist, clerk or scribe who occupied posts on the bottomless data chain below them, Ekharth and Lord Commander Udo had the knowledge required to solve all but the most dire of the Imperium's problems, or those that were to come. The abyssal infotombs of the Estate Imperium. The tithes chamber notarium. The ordozarchy of the Departmento Munitorum. The findings of inquiries and inquiries about inquiries, gathered in vellum mountains at the Officio Officium. Decades of back-dated threat assessments from the Logis Strategos, and vermillion-class strategic directives: Solar, Obscurus, Pacificus, Tempestus, Ultima and Extra-Galaxia. These were but a few of the byzantine institutions and divisions that answered to Ekharth and Udo's absolute authority. It wasn't as though the pair were not aware of the Ardamantuan atrocity. Even before the catastrophe, the Inquisition had brought the situation to Udo as part of a Critical Situation Packet. Ekharth was already well aware of the xenos species known as the Chromes in the form of the damage their encroachment was doing: missed tithes and trade disruptions.

After Ardamantua – as one xenos threat was exchanged for another – little changed for Ekharth and the Lord Commander. The orks had always been a threat. The Lord High Admiral's fleets were engaged in actions on the frontier space of the Imperium, defending worlds and trade routes from junkers, freebooting greenskins and upstart warlords declaring wars from warp-spewed space hulks. Indeed, beyond being dropped into such internecine border wars with the greenskins, Verreault – the new Lord Commander

Militant of the Astra Militarum – had inherited the Emperor's bastion amongst the stars only to find it already thoroughly committed to crusades and long-standing strategic engagements. Q'orl Swarmhood expansions. A Segmentum Solar-grazing hrud migration. Expeditionary fleets from the Nadirax Republic. Coreward appearances of the aggressive Biel-Tan craftworld. Carnivorous trans-plants mounting seed-invasions of Imperial systems surrounding the Nepenthis death world. Tarellian mercenary movements in the Phidas sector. The Kindred. The Xerontian Similisworn. The horrific resurgence of the Ubergast. Data continued to flood in from the various theatres and while Abel Verreault was eager that all threats received due attention, troops and materiel, response times were glacial. The Lord Commander Militant was often working with reports that were months out of date. Troop movements arrived to find xenos threats long eradicated. Some simply disappeared into the embrace of alien forces that had grown many times in magnitude since their deployment. Others found themselves sent astronomical distances to incorrect coordinates, finding nothing but dead space, wasted opportunity and relief in equal measure.

While some would later deem the Lord Commander Militant's inexperience in both the galactic theatre and the daedal politics of the Imperial Palace a factor in a catastrophe both unfolding and unappreciated, others would lay responsibility at the doors of the lords Udo and Ekharth. Only they truly had the pieces of the puzzle in their hands. Their blindness came not of inexperience, but of veteran pedantry. Amongst the dire threats already presented to

the Imperium, the myriad planetary tragedies and enemies innumerable – the evolving calamity heralded by the
Ardamantuan Atrocity was but one atrocity among many.

'A toast: to Beta-Novax...'

'...Fleur-de-Fides.'

'Beta-Novax was yesterday.'

'To Fleur-de-Fides, then.'

Resplendent in Navy dress uniform, Admiral Lansung
was bold and broad. His jacket was the blue of the deepest
oceans and the golden waterfalls of his epaulettes tumbled
from his thick shoulders. He parted the gathering like a capital ship on manoeuvres before joining Lord Commander
Udo and Ekharth at the Ecclesiarch's altar. Fraters moved
through the group of significants, handing out fortified
amasec and attending to the gathering's petty conveniences.
One by one, the Twelve approached the Anesidoran altar,
where Ecclesiarch Mesring delivered a blessing. Dipping
his chubby digits into the ash of incense, Mesring used his
thumb and finger to smear an aquila on the foreheads of
the presented worthies.

About them, the wolfish Wienand circled. She had respect-
fully left her bodyguard at the chapel archway and now she
watched and drifted, her eyes narrowing sharply beneath
her precisely cropped fringe. She absently took a glass of
amasec from a passing frater and exchanged greetings with
the Paternoval Envoy Helad Gibran without looking.

Wienand went through the motions. She drank in celebration of the feast day. She took her blessing. She bore her
soot sigil. All the time the Inquisitor was watching. Thinking. Reaching determination. The Imperium was ailing

and vulnerable to attack. The great men and women of the Imperium before her had grown like a cancer about their responsibilities. The Inquisition was the cure. They would surgically trim the tumorous lethargy and self-interest from the hallowed halls of the Imperial Palace in order to save the body politic. Strategies were in play. Pressure was being directed. Wheels turned within wheels, taking the Imperium in the right direction.

She looked up at the stained-glass representation of the God-Emperor behind Mesring and the attendant savant-priests that never left his side. It was her job – her sacrosanct duty – to further the Inquisition's myriad interventions and keep the Imperium on the right track. She despised surprises. She prided herself on being the most informed personage in the chamber, and wished to remain that way.

Surprises had a horrible way of manifesting in such meetings, however. In meetings of the Senatorum and of course, the meetings of members' agents in the darkness of hive basement sections and underlevels. Wienand was still breaking in Raznick, her new bodyguard. Her former escort-operative's smashed body had been dicovered in the bowels of a Tashkent mag-lev terminal. He had underestimated his quarry. It had served as a useful reminder to Wienand not to underestimate hers.

Her predacious movements were not lost on another of the chapel's predators. As Mesring's priests and fraters fell to prayer and the Ecclesiarch joined the rest of the Twelve, he was met with commiserations and faux-concern over the loss of the shrineworlds of the Jeronimus Fyodora cluster and the cardinal world of Mesring's own ordination: Fleur-de-Fides. Some dangers, like the unfolding greenskin crisis in the rimward sectors, were obvious. Some dangers liked to remain hidden. Some hid in plain sight. One thing was certain: the Anesidoran Chapel of the Imperial Palace, clouded with the lethal ambitions of both predators and prey, was one of the most dangerous places in the galaxy.

SEVEN

Terra – the Ecclesiarchal Palace

Mesring had spent most of the journey from the Imperial Palace in private devotions aboard his sacerdotal skiff. The skiff was essentially a floating, fortified basilica, garrisoned by zealot forces of the Frateris Templar. Its nest of spires, minarets and steeples were carried above the ancient urban sprawl of the southern continent on anti-gravitic drives. Its progress past the colossal accretion of Hive Vostok was stately and honoured by the thousands of preachers lighting incense beacons atop shell-shrines built into western face of the hive exterior. The Ecclesiarch briefly appeared at the observation balcony in the trappings of his office to acknowledge the half-million parishioners risking their lives in the creaking shrines to catch a glimpse of the High Lord. He took refreshment and rejuvenant in his private quarters, before purification and then meetings with the Pontifex Luna on matters of cult importance and Arch-Confessor Yaroslav over revisions to his already considerable security detail.

As the sacerdotal skiff made its final approach through

a corridor of cloudscraping bell towers, the Ecclesiarchal Palace rang with booming devotions. Banners and pennants streamed in the high-altitude winds and the smoke from feast day fires briefly engulfed the skiff. Below the roar of the anti-gravity engines, the courtyards and squares between the temple complexes and cathedrals were swarming with armies of fraters at prayer. Preachers and pontiffs creed-thumped their way through the ranks, shaking their ceremonial staffs and reading from ornate copies of the *Lectitio Divinatus* with priestly passion. Once again, Mesring presented himself in the full ceremonial regalia of the Ecclesiarch and moved through a series of services, with each of the Cardinals Palatine attempting to outdo the last in his feast day celebration. Only at the close of Cardinal Gormanskee's final reading – that the Ecclesiarch slept through, his snores stifled by his savant-priests – was Mesring due to retire to his palace chambers.

Mesring bulldozed his way up the mountain of steps, the magnificence of his crozier clacking on the marble of each. As the Ecclesiarch went, trailing an entourage of vergers and sextons, crusader sentries of the Frateris Templar went down on armoured knees. Up and along the grand stairs a gauntlet of vestal choristers sang haunting hymns to carry the High Lord to his great, golden bed. As he passed a serene and pretty face that he liked, Mesring paused.

'My chambers,' he said, jabbing the shaft of his crozier at a vestal that had caught his jaundiced eye, 'to attend me at night prayers.' He let his gaze travel to the young woman next to her. 'You, my child, get to attend my chambers at dawn.'

Both postulants beamed their appreciation at the special selection, having little idea of the kind of attendance the Ecclesiarch required from them. As Mesring ascended the last of the steps he allowed his savant-priests to take his mitre, staff and robes from his repugnant body.

Two auspex arches and Frateris Templar sentinel posts later, the Ecclesiarch barked, 'Just one!' The eruption prompted the gaggle of ushers, aides and savant-priests to peel away, either to their own miserable cells or to make preparations for the High Lord's morning requirements. As Mesring walked through the ornate archway of his grand chamber, with its antiquities and private opulence, he handed his remaining priest further layers of cermonial vestments. By the time he reached the septrewood table bearing the basin and pitcher of holy water, the Ecclesiarch was down to his undergown and rings. In silence the savant-priest deposited the garments on a nearby stand.

'Would you have me wait half the night on your tardiness, sir?' Mesring berated, prompting the priest to pour the water from the pitcher and into the marble bowl. The Ecclesiarch offered the priest his hands, at which the savant bowed and reverently kissed the pudgy backs of both. 'All right, all right,' Mesring grumbled impatiently.

The priest fell to removing the rings from Mesring's fat fingers and depositing them on a pair of sculpted, marble hands. Upon completion of this exercise, Mesring placed his hands in the basin and washed his weary face. He snatched a towel from the attendant priest and dabbed his features dry. As the Ecclesiarch scrunched the hand towel up and prepared to toss it back at the savant, he found the priest admiring one of his many extravagant rings of office.

'How dare you!' Mesring rumbled, bringing the back of his hand up to correct the attendant priest. 'Damned insolence,' he marvelled as the priest proceeded to try the ring on for size.

The savant-priest's own arm came up with astonishing speed and violence. Within moments the priest had the hand Mesring was threatening to slap him with in a horrific lock. The Ecclesiarch's features contorted beneath the fat of his face. The slightest twist of the priest's grip shot agony through the High Lord's trembling carcass.

The priest admired the Ecclesiarch's ring on the forefinger of his other hand. It was crafted in the likeness of the Adeptus Ministorum's holy symbol, inset with a tiny skull. The skull's eyes burned red, indicating that the ring was primed. Grabbing Mesring by one of his many chins, the priest forced him back to the cold marble of the wall. Mesring struggled but then, as the priest twisted his arm further, subsided with a pained groan.

The priest tapped his ring-adorned forefinger against the Ecclesiarch's throat. 'Beautiful,' he said simply, admiring the digital lasweapon. 'Jokaero, no?'

Mesring managed a terrified nod. 'Careful now,' the priest warned. 'I wouldn't want you to slit your own throat. Such craftsmanship should be employed in defence of your continued existence, not be the instrument of its ending. I'm sure you agree.'

This time Mesring signalled such agreement with the slow closing and opening of his yellowing eyes.

'Who are you?' Mesring hissed through his agonies. 'What do you want?'

'Who am I?' the savant-priest repeated – the savant-priest who had been chief attendant to the Ecclesiarch for decades. Who had been privy to his appetites and secrets. Who had attended on Mesring on board the sacerdotal skiff on the journey from the Imperial Palace. Who had assisted the Ecclesiarch in the bestowing of blessings upon the High Lords themselves in the Anesidoran Chapel. 'And what do I want?'

The priest seemed to move something around in his mouth and then proceeded to bite down hard. Mesring watched in horror as the priest's face began to tic and to tremble. Like a stone cast into a still pool, his features rippled. A ghastly transformation took place before the Ecclesiarch's fearful eyes. Long, grey hair rained to the marble floor along with clumps of the priest's tangled beard. False lenses ran down the imposter's cheeks like tears and a plastek film that had covered the priest's cracked and aged lips peeled away and fell to the floor like a strip of dry skin. With the localised polymorphine losing effect and the transformation complete, Mesring beheld his uninvited guest.

'Vangorich...'

'Yes.'

Face-to-face with his foe, some of Mesring's accustomed bluster returned.

'This is an outrage,' the Ecclesiarch seethed. 'The High Lords will hear of this!'

'No,' Drakan Vangorich, Grand Master of the Officio Assassinorum, told him with absolute certainty. 'You asked me a moment ago what I wanted. What I want right now, your eminence, is for you to shut that interminable hole in your face. For if you do not, I shall save your shoulders the further responsibility of bearing the weight of your head. I shall then have one of the many operatives I have planted in your organisation, studying your behaviour and mannerisms, wear your flesh and assume *your* responsibilities. Am I understood?'

Mesring considered the Grand Master's words and once again confirmed his understanding with his eyes.

'Here is what I need you to do,' Vangorich told him. 'You will contact Lord Commander Udo and have him convene another unscheduled meeting of the Twelve. *Just* the Twelve.'

'And why would I do that?' Mesring said.

'Ah, ah,' Vangorich reminded him, tapping his finger and digital weapon against the Ecclesiarch's throat. 'I do not want to be invited, but you can wager your life that I will be in there. Just like I was today.'

'I...'

The Grand Master raised his dark eyebrows. 'I'd need a good reason,' Mesring said, 'to justify that.'

'You have one,' Vangorich returned. 'You will tell them that you slept uneasily tonight. That the loss of the Jeronimus Fyodora shrine worlds weighed heavily on your mind and that you have taken the destruction of the Fleur-de-Fides cardinal world as a punishment – as a sign. An indication of the God-Emperor's dissatisfaction with the High Lords' present course of action in the rimward sectors.'

'I will not take the Emperor's name in vain,' Mesring hissed, 'and cheapen my faith with such falsehoods.'

'You will,' Vangorich insisted. 'You do already. Every day. Remember to whom you speak, Ecclesiarch. I have been your shadow for longer than you knew you had one. You will declare a War of Faith. You will raise frater militias and mobilise your Templar forces. Your priests across the segmentum will preach this from the pulpits. This will all be done under a banner of sacred vengeance. The priests and people of Fleur-de-Fides will be avenged. You will use your influence with the Lord High Admiral – in light of the Ardamantuan Atrocity, other devastations on the edge of the segmentum, and your War of Faith – to have him recall his fleets, armadas and flotillas from the diversion of border actions and campaign crusades. To ensure the new Lord Commander Militant and committed Astra Militarum forces have the full support of Navy warships and troop carriers. To redeploy our assets across the segmentum in anticipation of xenos invasion. These greenskin successes, their barbaric new technologies, this self-named Beast: these all add up to a credible threat, not to a single world or sector but to the very core. The Imperium is in clear and present danger.'

'You are not qualified to make that determination,' Mesring replied. 'And neither am I.'

'True,' Vangorich admitted. 'But there are those among us who are. Those who know and have always known more about this threat to our Imperial sovereignty amongst the stars. They are fearful. I look to their fear for guidance.'

'Then take some comfort from their interest and expertise,' the Ecclesiarch said. 'If they act, then why need we?'

'You, Udo, Lansung – your inaction is defined by political advantage. They act in spite of you, but to no lesser advantage. Terrible things are done in the name of necessity. Besides – I don't have reason to trust any of you. You will do these things I ask not because I have asked you. Not because I have threatened. You will do them because it is your duty. It is your hallowed responsibility to look to the safety and sanctity of the Emperor and His dominion. That is your only reason for being, Ecclesiarch.'

'Lansung is his own man,' Mesring insisted. 'He will not allow his ambitions to be thwarted. I won't be able to convince him to abandon wars he is already fighting. He will not break up his armadas. I can't–'

'You can and you will,' Vangorich warned. 'Many claim you to be your own man also, with power and boundless ambition. Yet here I am, using what I have to apply pressure in the right places. You will do the same. Use what you have with Lansung and find a way.'

'Why not remove Lansung?' Mesring suggested. 'If he's the problem, assassinate and replace him instead. Leave me out of this.'

'As always, I will do what I must,' the Grand Master admitted. 'But if the segmentum is under threat from invasion, we are going to need Admiral Lansung and his strategic experience. It might surprise you to learn this, your eminence, but I don't really want to kill anybody. But as I said: sometimes terrible things are done in the name of necessity.'

'Say I agree to this,' Mesring said with gravity. 'Say, for the sake of argument that I even agree with a recall strategy. This degenerate xenos Beast, after all, is decimating my worlds too. What's in it for me?'

Vangorich gave the Ecclesiarch a look of smouldering scorn and disgust. His lips tightened.

'Why, my lord Mesring... you get to live,' Vangorich told him. The Assassin became calmer and more dangerous with the Ecclesiarch's every incendiary suggestion. 'A few minutes ago I placed a toxin of unrivalled and agonising lethality in contact with your skin.' Mesring frowned. 'The devotion of a reverent kiss.'

Mesring looked from Vangorich's lips to the backs of his hands, then to the floor where the plastek strip bearing the toxin lay curled and abandoned after the Assassin's transformation.

'You poisoned me?' Mesring wheezed, trying to catch his breath.

'You have three days to meet my demands,' Vangorich told him. 'Three days to meet with the High Lords, to use your leverage with Lansung – to have him issue the recall. Three days until you die on your knees, bleeding from your ears, nose and eyeballs, praying for a mercifully swift and pain-less death you don't deserve from the God-Emperor you have served so very poorly. Upon successful completion of my demands, one of my operatives will deliver to you the antidote. If you fail, there will be no such need to do so.'

Vangorich released Mesring, before slipping the Eccle-siarch's digital weapon from his finger.

'I only have your word that I've been poisoned,' Mesring said weakly.

'Or that there's an antidote if you have,' Vangorich reminded him with chill certainty. 'Think of it this way: you put the same trust in me as I put in you.'

'You said that you didn't trust any of us.'

Vangorich dropped the Jokaero ring into the basin of holy water. He smiled and shrugged his shoulders. He brought up the hood on his priestly robe and sank down into its darkness before walking away.

Mesring's fat face was a nest of fury and confusion. Scrabbling through the water in the bowl, the Ecclesiarch found his weapon-ring and slid it onto his little finger. Pointing the weapon at Vangorich's presented back, the High Lord thought on the toxin working its way through the pores of his skin, through his blood and soaking slowly through his internal organs. He thought on the potential antidote in Drakan Vangorich's possession. The Ecclesiarch lowered his hand in defeat, and his eyes with it.

'Three days,' Vangorich's voice echoed about the Ecclesiarch's cavernous private chambers. Mesring looked up, but the Grand Master of Assassins was gone.

EIGHT

Incus Maximal / Malleus Mundi – orbital

Astropath Orm de Zut pulled himself through the module hatch and allowed his frail, green-robed frame to drift through the crowded weightlessness of the compartment. He wore a pair of tinted goggles to hide the empty sockets of his eyes, which, combined with his spindly frame, gave the astropath the appearance of an insect. He clutched a suckle-flask of low-grade amasec to his chest and allowed a lho-stick to drizzle smoke in his wake.

He negotiated the module in silence, inhaling through the narrow slits of his nostrils before exhaling through the grim line of his mouth. With one hand, the blind savant groped and pulled himself past various datamat, holomat and automat servitors who were wired into their observation cradles. Finding a corner of the compartment not drowning in cables, surveillance equipment or Adeptus Mechanicus priest-personnel and servitors, de Zut settled in an alcove, bobbing about in the zero gravity.

'Master de Zut,' Notatio Logi Lutron Vydel addressed the astropath. 'You are intoxicated, sir – again.' There was no hint of accusation or displeasure in the adept's static-laced voice, no wrinkle of vexation in the ebony flesh of his hood-framed face. As ranking priest on the Addendus~727 Broad Spectra Adeptus Mechanicus Signum-Station, the notatio logi was not given to such emotional indulgence. It was simply a statement of recorded fact. Like a hump-shuttle pilot on a outpost, only required during the cycle changeover of arrival and exodus, de Zut was bored, under-employed and without distraction.

De Zut said nothing.

'My brother adept is reminding you of your responsibil-ities,' Lexmechanic Autegra Ziegl said, turning away from the rune banks built into almost every surface of the com-partment. She reached past the astropath. Nudging him to one side in the zero gravity, the lexmechanic adjected several plungers and dials. The outline of her cranial cogi-tator was like a research installation built into an asteroid, its unit-accretions dominating her shaven head.

'This is the Omnissiah's work,' she said. 'His loyal serv-ants work hard to compile statistics and testimonia for the astro-telecommunication data package.'

'To Mars,' de Zut said, putting one hand across his chest in a mock salute while raising his suckle-flask.

'It would be an unacceptable waste of time, resources and data,' Notatio Logi Vydel added, 'if the package were not to reach the Fabricator General's choralis diagnostiad.'

'It would,' de Zut agreed, taking another slug of amasec.

'Which is why I've opened a file on your fitness for such

an important duty,' Vydel told the astropath with cold indifference.

'A file,' de Zut repeated. 'Honoured.' Again, he raised the flask.

'Auspexmechanic Kelso Tollec has been identified as best qualified to monitor your competence,' Vydel said. Tollec turned his hooded face from the data-pulsing rune banks and refocused his ocular-quad of bionics on the astropath.

De Zut picked tobacco from his thin lips.

'I can make Adept Tollec's service record and signum-specifications available for your perusal, if you wish,' said Ehrlen Ohmnio.

Ohmnio was an officious transmechanic with an annoyingly cheerful face-mask. De Zut took a long drag on his lho-stick before flooding the crowded surveillancia module with silky smoke and reaching for a plunger set in the compartment ceiling.

'Please don't touch that,' Vydel said. The logi was very particular about the signum-station's equipment.

De Zut gave him the dark lenses of his goggles and yanked down hard on the handle. The compartment rumbled as a metal blast screen lowered to reveal the thick armourglass of the module's observation port. The searing ice-white glare of the Incus Maximal and Malleus Mundi forge-worlds dominated the void beyond. The surfaces of the pair were blotched with the black clouds of planetary destruction. Between them sat the rusted, clinker-plate body of an armoured moon: a greenskin abomination that rained swarms of invasion craft down on the frozen planets. Hanging above the decimation of xenos conquest was a flotilla of

Adeptus Mechanicus ark ships and supertransports receiving the last of the forge-world survivors.

'This is what I am referring to, master astropath,' Vydel told him, without the suggestion of annoyance or inconvenience de Zut's actions might have provoked. 'Such wilful behaviour necessitates monitoring. I expected more of your kind. That was my mistake – after all, you are flesh and flesh is weak.' The logi turned to his auspexmechanic. 'Tollec, I want scan coverage, augur arrays and vox-monitoring intensified by forty per cent in line of sight quadrants. Particularly those occupied by Mechanicus contingents. Without filters, we might have emitted some optical or energy signature of our position.'

'Scanning,' the auspexmechanic said.

'I understand why our surveillance needs to remain hidden from the enemy,' de Zut acknowledged. 'But your own people and priesthood? You've let them just die up to now anyway. Soon there won't be anyone left to detect your presence.'

'Master de Zut,' Vydel said. 'Are you familiar with our Third Law of Universal Variance?'

'He will not comprehend,' Autegra Ziegl said with confidence.

'It is called the Bystander Paradox,' Vydel continued, 'and it states that whatever the Machine God's servant observes, he affects. The magos metallurgicus' involvement in an experiment might threaten to change its chemical outcome. An alien life form might behave differently under the gaze of a magos biologis than it would in its natural environment. A patient might stifle pain or embarrassing symptoms in the presence of a magos physic. You see, this signum-station is under strict orders – from the Fabricator General himself. Covertly observe. Record. Document. Do not interact. That is our solemn responsibility. And it is your solemn responsibility to send the sum total of our data and observations back to Mars.'

'Solemn responsibility?' the astropath repeated back. 'What about our responsibility to those people?'

'Their loss has been weighed and measured against future gains,' Vydel replied.

'And what of the losses on other worlds?' de Zut spat back morosely. 'While you coldly catalogue the slaughter of the Machine God's servants, what of the mortis-cries of the dozen Imperial worlds I have intercepted? Mortis-cries of dying billions that I am bound by ancient decrees of my own order to report on, but that your surveillance protocols forbid?'

'I calculate that to be a burden, master astropath,' Lutron Vydel said. 'But a necessary one. We cannot allow enemies – xenos or domestic – to learn of our surveillance. I understand that the mortis-cries might have tested you...'

'These deaths are but data to you,' de Zut said grimly. 'You can close your blast screens so that you might avoid looking down on your losses. I have no such screen. I live each and every one: in here,' the astropath said, slapping his palm against his temple.

'I repeat,' Vydel said, 'we acknowledge the burden of such mortis-cries.'

'And of the astrotelepathic distress calls to have reached us?' de Zut interrupted. 'What of the living, priest? Thirsk's World? Aguilarn Tertius? Eidolica? The Verge Worlds?

Fifty-One Xerxi? Port Sanctus? Undine? What of those we could save by breaking your precious Law of Universal Variance? Those who might be saved by others, if you only allow me to pass on their communications? We might be the only ones to have intercepted such calls for assistance.'

'Out protocols are clear,' Vydel said, unaffected by the astropath's entreaties. 'We are authorised to send one communication. One communication containing our evidence and findings. Observations of enemy conquest strategies, the workings of xenos technologies and the relative successes or failures of victim-worlds to repel invasions. One communication signalling the signum-station's readiness for extraction and redeployment. These billions you feel for do not perish in vain. The Fabricator General will learn much from their annihilation.'

De Zut pushed himself back into the corner of the compartment, defeated by the cold logic of the tech-priests. Unclipping herself from her observation cradle, Autegra Ziegl allowed herself to drift upwards. Reaching out, she depressed the ceiling plunger, initiating the hydraulic closure of the port blast screen. She had no words of comfort for the astropath. Such capacity had long been surgically sliced from what was left of her organic brain, but she watched de Zut with brazen curiosity as he shook his head and took a long, hard drink from his suckle-flask.

'I don't understand you,' he mouthed before again returning to the zero-gravity teat on the flask.

Ziegl turned to her notatio logi master.

'Perhaps we should send the intelligence package now,' she said.

Kelso Tollec turned his ocular-quad on the lexmechanic. 'What of the data-loss? The analytical deficiencies?'

'We would be failing both our Fabricator General and the Omnissiah,' Erhlen Ohmnio said, his cheerful face-mask unchanged.

'Master de Zut is under your monitorance,' Ziegl put to Tollec. 'Can you vouch that he will be able to send communication following the destruction of the cryoforge-worlds? That could take days. It could take weeks. How many more mortis-cries will he intercept in that time?'

The auspexmechanic considered, then admitted to Vydel, 'Master de Zut's capabilities and willingness to serve the Machine God with his talents diminish with his intoxication and deteriorating state of mind. He is apparently unsuited for the isolation of surveillance service on a signum-station. I calculate a twenty-six point four five per cent chance that he will abuse his talents and relay the astrotelepathic messages he has received – thereby invalidating our surveillance and possibly betraying our position to an enemy.'

'Better to send the package incomplete and be of some use to the diagnostiad, than not have it reach them at all,' Vydel said.

'But the protocols...' Erhlen Ohmnio restated.

'Sub-protocols allow for adaptation in the face of an external threat to the sacred data,' Vydel insisted. 'An accident or enemy offensive, for example. I am willing to interpret Master de Zut's weakness of the flesh as such an external threat.'

Taking the flask of amasec from Orm de Zut, Vydel looked from the defeated astropath to his lexmechanic. 'Begin preparing the data we have for empyreal translation. Master de Zut will sober up and send our findings to Mars, where, Omnissiah willing, they shall aid the Fabricator General and his choralis diagnostiad in their holy cerebrations.'

NINE

Mars – Olympica Fossae Titan Assembly Yards

The Adeptus Mechanicus haulage barge *Internuncia* gave an almighty creak as its landing claws touched down in red Martian dirt. Gone was the weightless indifference of the void. The forge-world's gravity asserted its authority, and the great vessel and its consignment cargo of colossal Titan parts reacquired their crushing cumbersomeness. The drop-freighter was a largely automated vessel, crewed by mummified servitors, servomat drones and robotic cargo loaders. It routinely ferried parts for repair and reconditioning between the Terran Titan depots and the Olympica assembly yards on the Red Planet, transported between the two by the articulated push-tug *Sumpter*, which was waiting obediently in orbit. The ranking crew member was a helms-mechanic, wired into the gargantuan craft's tiny cockpit, whose responsibility it was to pilot the barge between low orbit and the planetary surface.

As the massive bay doors opened and mechanised drones fell to the task of loading and offloading their precious cargo, a figure in dark robes broke the angularity of its cover. Not a servitor. Not a drone automaton. A stowaway. Striding down the mountainous ramp behind the broad tracks of cargo robots and between the heavy steps of power-lifter servo-mats, the figure's ample hood buried its features. It looked up briefly. Weak rays of early morning sunlight were feeling their way around the imposing architecture of the Olympus Mons forge temple: grand, functional, beautiful. Olympus Mons, forge of the ancients. Cult capital of the Adeptus Mechanicus. Seat of the Fabricator General of Mars. It was a magnificent sight, sitting, as it did, like a colossal crown of glowing chimneys, furnace stacks and temple towers atop the largest volcano in the Sol System. It was a reminder of the power wielded by the Machine God's servants in the galaxy. An empire allied, but still distinct from the Emperor's Imperium and ruled from the red majesty of Mars.

At the bottom of the ramp, the figure found a gathering in the great shadow of the haulage barge. A meeting of equally dark shapes, waiting to be convened. A meeting unseen and secret; a meeting of assassins and killers, with death warrants at a glance – for those unfortunate enough to observe such occurrences, by design or by accident, rarely saw the next sunrise.

As monotask machinery and augmented vat-slaves went about their unloading duties, the group presented themselves to the waiting figure. Two wore the red-robed pageantry of the Adeptus Mechanicus. Two more sported cloaks and masks of midnight black over muscle-hugging syn-skin and boots of the same colour. The fifth was hulking and naked, but for being entirely enclosed in a cryo-containment pod. The sarcophagus was positioned upright and steamed with methalon gas, creating a heavy mist that sank to the floor.

'Sleeper Cadre *Red Haven*: identify,' the figure ordered them.

The first of the false-Mechanicus figures stepped forwards and offered the haptic finger ports of her hand.

'Clementina Yendl, my lord,' the Assassin said. 'Temple Vanus.'

The figure took her hand in his gauntleted one and pierced her skin with a hypodermic palm spike. Painful though the experience was, the Assassin didn't flinch. Holding her hand still, the figure turned his gauntlet and examined the data scrolling across a miniature runescreen inlaid at the wrist.

'Clementina Yendl, Temple Vanus – Red Haven, confirmed,' the figure said.

The procedure was repeated. 'Mariazet Isolde, Temple Callidus – Red Haven, confirmed,' the figure said to the other forge-world impersonator – her red-robed disguise benefiting further from a bronze mask, authentic cybernetic augmentation and the stench of oil and spoiling flesh.

'Saskine Haast, Temple Vindicare and Sklera Verraux, Temple Vindicare – Red Haven, confirmed,' the figure said, identifying the pair of stealth-suited markswomen.

Placing his hand on the side of the upright cryo-containment pod, the figure interfaced with a hypodermic port and drew blood from the occupant.

'Tybalt the Abolitiate,' Yendl of Temple Vanus informed the visitor.

The figure inspected his gauntlet.

'Temple Eversor – Red Haven, confirmed,' he said finally.

While the Vindicare markswomen retained their masks and Tybalt the Abolitiate remained reassuringly cryo-confined, both Yendl and Isolde drew back their hoods. Isolde disconnected her Mechanicus Protectorate honour mask with the hand that had not been replaced by a mind-impulse-controlled implant weapon, to reveal a pallid but beautiful face. The flaskless plasma gun glowed beneath the Callidus Assassin's cloak.

Yendl was a bookish woman, lacking in the surgically refined allurements favoured by many female operatives of the temples. Beauty, for many Assassins, was simply another weapon in their varied arsenals, but Yendl had elected to remain unremarkable by comparison with her cadre companions. Framed between the greying braids on the sides of her head and within the holo-lenses of her spectacles, however, the infocyte's eyes burned with dark, destructive intelligence. She held an armoured data-slate under one arm, a weighty intel-log that trailed rune cables and data-feeds back under her robes.

'My lord,' Yendl insisted. 'If you don't mind.'

The figure nodded.

'And you are right to insist,' he told her as ghostly overlays rippled through the display of her holo-spectacles and the dots of face recognition beams pulsed from devices built into her frames onto the stranger's face. The figure managed a grim patience during the brief scan.

'Well?' Sklera Verraux said through the vox-filter of her mask. Both Verraux and her sister sniper had tensed at the delay in Yendl's usually swift cogitations.

'Drakan Vangorich,' Yendl said finally.

'Grand Master – Officio Assassinorum: confirmed,' Drakan told them.

With the exception of the monster Tybalt, who physically couldn't know he was in the presence of the highest ranking member of their order, the Red Haven sleeper cadre fell to an obedient knee.

'Grand Master,' Yendl said, 'if we had known that you were coming to Mars in person...'

'...then I hope you would not have wasted time on ceremony,' Vangorich told his Assassins. 'Are we secure?'

'Yes, my lord,' the Vanus Assassin assured him. 'I have had all vox, pict and identifeeds out of this section – surface and orbital – phage-blocked.'

Vangorich nodded: 'I grace the Red Planet's presence because the intelligence you have gathered is of grave importance, not only to me and the Officio but also the Imperium. The guardian-vigilance of Assassin sleeper cadres like your own has never been more important. Not since the Great Heresy have the actions of so few endangered so many.'

'Of course, Grand Master,' Yendl replied. She knew better than to ask for more details.

'Now,' Vangorich said, 'to Fabricator General Kubik's transgressions.'

'This encrypted log contains our gathered evidence and observations in full, Grand Master,' Yendl said, disconnecting the security data-slate from her cabling and offering the log to Vangorich. 'In short, my lord, the Fabricator General has been keeping valuable intelligence from the Senatorum.'

'What kind of intelligence?' the Grand Master demanded.

'Results and observations gathered by his priests and adepts regarding the spread of xenos species in the rimward sectors,' Yendl said. 'The so-called Chromes. The Fabricator General has had his *magi biologis* and artisans trajectorae criss-crossing the segmentum, collating data from maximum-security laboratoria, observation posts and signum-stations.'

'Where are these Adeptus Mechanicus installations?'

'They are spread across the outer rim sectors, Grand Master,' Yendl replied, 'covertly monitoring worlds that have reported infestations of the Chrome vermin-species – including many citing minor outbreaks and Stage One planetary intrusions.'

Vangorich swore under his breath. 'Kubik was presented with the Critical Situation Packet regarding the Chromes but refuted its threat credibility. All the while establishing his network of observation posts.'

'The Fabricator General himself could be considered a credible threat,' Yendl offered.

Vangorich slowly shook his head. 'Kubik wasn't wrong – logical bastard. The Chromes themselves aren't the issue. It's the predator species driving them corewards. No Critical Situation Packet was presented for them.'

'No, my lord.'

'Wienand must have been spitting blood,' the Grand Master said, half to himself. 'Was Kubik the source of the Inquisition's initial information?'

'Affirmative,' Yendl said, 'in the first instance.'

'Then when the Fabricator General realised that he was onto something significant and beneficial to the Adeptus

Mechanicus, he cut her off,' Vangorich reasoned further. 'He buried her Critical Situation Packet: the threat assessment his servants had helped to compile. Machines...' Vangorich marvelled. 'Wienand?'

'The lady inquisitor is a frequent visitor to Mars,' Mariazet Isolde answered. 'She carelessly leaves her operatives here. They are currently being monitored.'

'Would you prefer us to take more direct action, my lord?' Saskine Haast asked.

The Grand Master shook his head: 'Avoid entanglements with the Inquisition, if possible. If it isn't possible, then do what you do best.' With a nod, Vangorich returned his thoughts to Kubik. 'You said these stations are gathering data covertly?' he prompted Yendl.

'They still are,' the Temple Vanus operative informed her master. 'Encrypted astrotelepathic intelligence packages arrive daily for the attention of the Fabricator General and his choralis diagnostiad.' Vangorich lifted his hood in question. 'The extensive coven of priests and magi he has convened to look to the problems and opportunities created by the xenos threat in the rimward sectors,' Yendl clarified.

'What of Adeptus Mechanicus forge-worlds?'

'Installation personnel are under strict orders not to interfere with what the Fabricator General calls the *Grand Experiment*. He has not warned or attempted to spare his own servants.'

'Machines...' Vangorich repeated. 'Was the intercept world, Ardamantua, being monitored?'

'Kubik continues to recieve astrotelepathic updates from the system,' Yendl said.

'But the fleet was destroyed above Ardamantua.'

'The reports are sent from a secure laboratorium aboard the *Subservius,* a Martian survey brig masquerading as an Imperial Fists fleet tender. Records show that the vessel was engaged in a supply run during the gravitic disturbances on Ardamantua, but she had in fact been ordered by the ranking priest on board, Artisan Trajectorae Van Auken, to haul off in advance of the gravity storm. This was deemed necessary to make observations of the enemy's arrival.'

'The Mechanicus had an early warning system for the gravity storms, before Ardamantua?' Vangorich pressed.

'Appearance of the vermin-species,' Yendl said, 'followed by auditory phenomena on a broadening range of frequencies, followed in turn by seismogravitic disturbances, increasing in magnitude. Their predictive system was established and trialled at Desh, Concorda Corona and Nostroya IV.'

'I don't recall these disasters being reported to the Senatorum,' Vangorich said.

'They predate Ardamantua, sir. In all likelihood,' Yendl said, 'their tragedies were reported as some other kind of phenomenon. These worlds are confirmed as dead, however. They are in the hands of the invader. Grand Master, may I have permission to speak candidly?'

'Granted, Assassin.'

'Our protocols for an action are very stringent,' Yendl put to him.

'And rightly so.'

'By the letter of those protocols,' Yendl said, 'have not the actions of the Fabricator General justified his termination?

He's withholding a wealth of essential information from the Senatorum and embarking on a course of action – individually determined – that might very well be putting the Imperium in grave danger. An action is justified, my lord. Some might argue warranted and necessary.'

'Unfortunately,' Vangorich told her, 'it is not as simple as that.'

'But, my lord, aren't the magnitude of these considerations beyond the politics of the Senatorum?'

'Nothing is beyond the politics of the Senatorum,' Vangorich said. 'I understand your impatience. The need to act. I too have done my time watching those deserving of death breathe on, unpunished, under my blade and in my sights. The Fabricator General's time will come, and he won't be alone. The fact is that as of this moment, with the core facing a xenos invasion of unprecedented proportions, we are going to need Kubik and the results of his Grand Experiment. Detest them as I might, the advantage the Martian priesthood are searching for might benefit us all.'

'Grand Master,' Yendl persisted cautiously. 'Forgive me my doubts, but I am not so sure. Beyond a diagnostic analysis of enemy strategic behaviours and the relative successes and failures of Imperial worlds to delay the invasion, it won't surprise you to learn that the principal interest the Adeptus Mechanicus has in these calamities is the technologies used to promote them.'

'Kubik is actively researching the xenos technologies?' Vangorich asked in slow and deliberate syllables.

'More than that, Grand Master,' Yendl told him. 'Kubik has several maximum security projects under excavation and construction beneath the surface of Mars. As yet, we have been unable to gain access to these projects. We know that one is located beneath the Noctis Labyrinth, with other larger excavations taking place at intervals below the Valles Marineris.'

'What is the Mechanicus building?' Vangorich demanded.

'We don't yet know, my lord,' Yendl admitted, 'but much of the data sent back to Mars from the secreted outposts and signum-stations focuses on the teleportation and vector technologies that the xenos use to transport their attack moons over sector-spanning distances.'

'Kubik wishes to learn the heretical secrets of this barbaric technology?' Vangorich said, before once again allowing his mind to dwell on the politics. 'Perhaps the Inquisition's interest in Kubik is less collaborative than the Fabricator General conceives.'

'My lord,' Yendl continued, 'with respect, you are not thinking broadly enough. We believe that the Fabricator General's interests lie not in what is best for the Imperium – but what is best for the Mechanicus. Kubik does not wish to learn the secrets of the xenos tech in order to destroy it or defend against it. He wishes to utilise it. Replicate it. Embrace its potential.'

'You're saying that...'

'I'm saying, my lord, that in the event of a threat to the inner core, to the Sol subsector – from the invader or anything else – he means to remove Mars from the path of annihilation.'

'Move the planet?' Vangorich said, his mind struggling with the enormity of the proposal.

'Save Mars,' Yendl said, 'and leave the Imperium to the ravages of the enemy.'

'Does he have these secrets?'

'Unknown, my lord. But if and when he does, beyond the defensive capabilities of such secrets, such techno-heretical wonders would make the Martian forge-world an intoler-able weapon.'

'Agreed,' Vangorich said finally. He turned with the intel-ligence log under one arm and ventured soberly back up the colossal ramp.

'My lord,' Yendl called after him, after a moment of recon-sideration. A little way up, the Grand Master of Assassins turned. 'Understand, sir, this is speculation. We have no direct evidence of the construction of such a heretical abomination.'

Vangorich cast his eyes bleakly across the sleeper cadre.

'Red Haven: Priority Primus,' the Grand Master said to them. 'Find some.'

TEN

Ardamantua

Ardamantua was a gravity-churned mess, a mass grave that had suffered tectonic upheaval. An aftermath of fresh earth and rotting bodies. It was fascinating.

Artisan Trajectorae Argus Van Auken was standing in a craterous hollow swarming with Mechanicus menials and seisomats taking readings and feeding the data back to the survey brig *Subservius*, which held position in low orbit above the expedition. Magi astrophysicus bombarded the ruined structure of the Ardamantuan crust with magna-sonic arrays and powerful pulse-scanners, the dishes and receivers of which were directed down into the ground.

As soon as the distress calls from the surface had faded and the colossal xenos attack moon disappeared – which had happened as swiftly as the abomination had arrived – the *Subservius* had returned. Argus Van Auken had come back at the head of a small army of data-ravenous priests and adepts, all intent on understanding the mechanics of the catastrophe. They busied themselves with experimentation and observation, all the while trampling xenos corpses – both common Chromes and *Veridi giganticus* – and the shredded remains of Mechanicus support staff, and the shattered yellow plate of fallen Imperial Fists, into the disturbed earth.

Only knowledge mattered. The xenos cadavers were fearfully imposing, even in death. The honourable Adeptus Astartes – torn to pieces in the enemy deluge – deserved better. Argus Van Auken was incapable of such distractions, however. His work benefited from a lack of such sentimentality. Some might describe it as a disability. Others, a superhuman ability. It had been Van Auken's cold logic that had held the *Subservius* on station, pursuing its observation protocols when lesser adepts like Magos Biologis Eldon Urquidex had urged the artisan to return and interfere with unfolding events. Perhaps it had been Urquidex's devotion to the science of the living that had burdened the priest with such weakness. Urquidex had watched the data-streams of doom return from the planet's surface. He saw an Adeptus Astartes Chapter on the brink of annihilation. He saw the physical perfection of the human form and a rich genetic history of conquest and supremacy on the cusp of extinction. He gave in to his baser, organic impulses and requested of Van Auken a last-minute retrieval.

The request was denied – and as the expedition's second-ranking priest, Urquidex received a citation for modus-unbecoming from the first. Van Auken reminded his colleague of the Third Law of Universal Variance: the Bystander Paradox. Urquidex had replied that they called it a paradox for a reason.

The alien Beast had unleashed its savage supremacy on Ardamantua and all those upon its surface. None had survived. Only the data – pure and true – remained. It was Van Auken's responsibility to see that the information found its way back to Mars where it might aid the Fabricator General in his service of the Machine God's will.

Striding through auspexmechanics and oscillamats that were monitoring the structural damage to the planetary depths, Van Auken ascended the hollow's slopes to find that Urquidex's survey crews had planted electrostatic rods in the mulched earth. About the artisan-primus, fields of static electricity had raised the dead. Hulking greenskin corpses were drifting a few feet above the ground on the crackling field, making examination of the bolt-ravaged specimens easier for the magos biologis and his genetor tech-adepts. The Beast's work on Ardamantua had been so absolute in its ferocity that there were no other remains to examine. The Space Marines and accompanying Adeptus Mechanicus personnel of the Ardamantuan purge had been hacked and blasted to pieces. The monsters had been possessed of a bottomless ferocity that seemed to infect the creatures even down to their diminutive slave and vermin forms.

Knocking the monstrous bodies into a telekinetic tumble, Van Auken's spindly form passed through the levitated carnage. But for the electromagnetic dampeners built into his torso, the artisan also would have floated effortlessly across the tormented earth. Skitarii from the Epsil-XVIII Collatorax stood sentinel among the sea of bodies, with their galvanic rifles cradled in bionic limbs. They had been assigned as expedition security and for use as execution squads, putting

down monstrosities that had not quite bled their formidable life away on the battlefield. Alpha Primus Orozko saw the approaching artisan-primus and marched to meet him.

'With me, magister, if you please,' Van Auken requested. The officer said nothing. Orozko wasn't much of a communicator, favouring binary for orders and transmissions. He simply fell in line behind the ranking priest.

'Magos,' Van Auken said as he entered a foil laboratory-pavilion. Neither Eldon Urquidex nor his surgeons and samplers looked up from the gargantuan carcass of the ork they were dissecting on the static field. Slabs of flesh and labelled alien organs floated about them. 'Magos,' the artisan-primus repeated. 'My teams have all but completed their documentation of the damage inflicted by the alien weapon.'

'And...?' the barrel-bodied Urquidex said, not taking his telescopic eyes off the brain of the beast he was carving up with a digit-mounted las-scalpel.

'The enemy's mastery of gravity manipulation and tele-portational vectors is considerable,' Van Auken said, his understatement devoid of wit or passion. The priest paused; his colleague had a habit of soliciting information when he should be delivering it. 'The gravitational aftershocks began to subside after the weapon removed itself from the system. Its disruptive influence endures, however, fading incrementally. It will be some time before gravito-planetary equilibrium is fully restored to this world.'

'Fascinating...'

'It is like nothing the Machine God's servants have documented before. It is a weapon the mere presence of which is a force of ultimate destruction. A blade that cuts without being drawn from its sheath; a bolt that blasts without leaving the barrel. If we are to achieve similar masteries, we must understand how the alien accomplishes such wonders. Scrutiny of the workings of their technology alone only reveals that it should not work at all. This is an unacceptable conclusion for our data packet.'

'Indeed,' Urquidex agreed.

'The Fabricator General demands better of us,' the artisan said.

'Always,' the magos replied absently.

'Magos,' Van Auken insisted, 'I must have your hypotheses.'

Urquidex looked up from the alien brain, his telescopic eyes retracting and refocusing.

'Why rush such important research?' the magos said with a withering gaze.

'There is a time for everything,' Van Auken said, 'and for everything a time.'

'Has this time been allocated for wastage?' Urquidex asked. 'Since it seems to be achieving little else.'

'The *Subservius* has been ordered on,' Van Auken insisted. 'We are to rendezvous with several signum-stations before moving corewards to establish observations above Macromunda.'

'To watch another unwarned world offered up before the alien for slaughter?' Urquidex said.

'You must learn to govern your sentimentality,' Van Auken instructed. 'Macromunda is no less a sacrifice than those genelings you experiment on in your laboratorium. These worlds would die anyway. We watch them die so that Mars might live. Now, enough of this. What observations can you add to the data packet? What is the secret of the xenos technology?'

Urquidex gave his superior the narrowing lenses of his telescopic eyes. Retracting the digit-scalpel into the tool-age of his bionic hand, the magos produced a pencil beam from his cranial arrangement, the red dot of which hovered across the artisan trajectorae's narrow forehead. Urquidex turned back to the xenos brain he had been working on.

'This structure here,' Urquidex said, indicating a bulbous feature at the brainstem that appeared like a bloom of fungus erupting from the base of a tree, 'governs the problem-solving faculties of the species – at least that is my theory.'

'Like you, I am a priest of Mars,' Van Auken reassured him. 'This is a xenos abomination – there are no certainties, only theories to be tested. Proceed, magos.'

'In many alien space-faring species, as well as our own,' Urquidex told him, 'such structures – dealing with inspiration, experimentation and technological develop-ment – occur in the frontal lobes.' Urquidex passed the dot across a comparatively redundant part of the creature's brain. 'Or the xenos equivalent thereof. In a race who have taken that crucial and technologically demanding step into a larger universe, you would expect this to be an area of recent evolutionary development.'

'Agreed.'

'Not so in *Veridi giganticus*,' the magos biologis said. 'It occurs in one of the most primitive parts of the organ.'

'But what does that mean?' Van Auken asked.

'It means that their technological mastery, being what it is, proceeds not from evolutionary, intellectual development as it has in humans and many other races. It has been a feature of their race from very early in their existence.'

'An accelerated development?' Van Auken hoped so. Acceleration could be modelled. Acceleration could be predicted.

'No,' Urquidex told him. 'Something primordial. A capability innate within their species. Their mastery of technology – including the gravitational and vector capabilities that you would wish to reproduce – is a natural ability. Not a product of some form of developed, higher order conception.'

'These conclusions will not please the Fabricator General,' Van Auken said.

'It is only a theory,' Urquidex said. 'Other priests at other conquest-sites may reach other conclusions.'

'Have you learned anything else?' Van Auken asked.

Urquidex turned and snapped on a hololithic projector that enveloped the monstrous brain in a fluxing field representation.

'What is that?' the artisan asked.

'Honestly?' the magos said, 'I don't know. I happened upon the frequency by accident. This is the barest manifestation of it, I can tell you that. It has been fading since biological cessation.'

'If you had to make an informed guess, magos?'

'Some kind of field or emanation,' Urquidex said. 'It seems to be coming from deep within the brain structure – again, an evolutionarily ancient feature.'

'Could it be psionic in nature?' Van Auken asked cautiously.

'Unknown,' Urquidex said with equal reservation, 'not my area of specialisation. However, watch this.'

Urquidex directed a pair of servitors into the foil tent. Between them they carried an alien weapon: some kind of barbaric chopping implement sporting a chain of revolving teeth like a chainsword. A brute motor was built into its ungainly shaft, the handle of which was scored with primitive glyphs and graffiti. The magos directed the drones to slip the savage weapon into the beast's death-stiffened grip, and lay the great shaft of the weapon and its murderous headpiece across the greenskin's open and organ-excavated chest.

'What are you doing?' Van Auken asked, as Urquidex directed a servomat to attach power couplings to the weapon's monstrous motor. 'Magos?'

'Clear...' Urquidex said, before instructing the servomat to supply power to the weapon from its own core.

The serrated chain of the chopper roared to life, the clunky machinery of its motor squealing and crunching, the gore of the Emperor's Angels spraying Van Auken from the monstrous weapon's thrashing teeth. The artisan stepped back and wiped the speckles of old blood from his face.

'Turn it off,' he commanded.

'As you wish,' Urquidex said, selecting an autopsy cleaver with a monomolecular edge from a rack of similarly macabre tools. Swinging the cleaver down with force, the magos chopped at the hulking wrist of the greenskin. It took a number of strikes, with the cleaver-blade biting through flesh and bone. With a final strike the claw-hand was separated from the meat of the arm – and the weapon chugged, bucked and died. Van Auken stepped back towards the creature with fresh interest.

'It still has power?'

'The problem isn't power,' Urquidex assured the artisan-primus. 'The weapon has suffered a malfunction, which isn't surprising given the poor quality of its construction and maintenance. I fear that this field – swiftly depleting and dissipating after death – in some way aids the crude workings of such creations.'

'But what of technologies not in direct contact with the xenos?'

'Unknown. The weapon was a simple demonstration with a cadaver-specimen,' Urquidex said. 'I have not observed the field's properties in a living organism. I don't know for sure that the field is responsible.'

'If it was, could the field be replicated?'

'Unknown. Not my specialisation.'

Artisan Van Auken took a moment to process this new data.

'These are important findings,' Van Auken said. 'They must reach Mars without delay.'

Urquidex watched the artisan process more than just the findings. Van Auken, who scorned the display of emotions in his colleagues, had difficulty keeping pride in his expedition's work from his gaunt face. Greed followed as an afterthought. Greed for power, recognition and influence. It was his name and designation as artisan-primus that would accompany the data packet to Mars. He who would be recalled to serve in the sacred ranks of the Fabricator General's diagnostiad.

'There is something else,' Urquidex said, shaking Van

Auken from his machinations.

'Proceed,' the artisan trajectorae encouraged, eager for more revelations.

'I have gene-typed the creature and a sample of its kind,' the Magos Biologis said, 'and cross-referenced our findings with the data-vaults aboard the *Subservius*.'

'And what did you discover?' Van Auken urged.

'They all have the same origin, genetically speaking,' Urquidex said. 'With some more work, we should be able to narrow it down to a particular area of the galaxy. Perhaps even a single world.'

A burst of binary cant from Alpha Primus Orozko interrupted the pair of priests. An alpha of the Epsil-XVIII Collatorax had reported to the primus. Urquidex and Van Auken turned, and Orozko prompted the subordinate to report.

'Artisan-primus,' the tribunus said. 'The augurmats have discovered life signs and designation signatures in quadrant four. They're weak but verified and coming from beneath the ground.'

'Survivors?' Eldon Urquidex dared to hope.

'Witnesses,' Van Auken corrected him, 'to the end of a world. Take us to them.'

The alpha led his commander and the two priests through the floating carnage about the magos' field of electrostatic rods. Beyond the static, the sampling crews and the skitarii standing sentinel, the alpha took them to a small excavation. A cordon of gathered Collatorax, augurmats and a servitor dig-team parted to admit the artisan-primus, and a medicae servitor looked up from its work at the tech-priests' arrival.

A pair of stretcher-bearing servitors carried the remains of an ashen priest from the excavation site. He was clad in the robes of the Mechanicus, besmirched with Ardamantuan earth, but had suffered the horrific injuries of battle. His legs were missing, hacked away by some brute weapon of war. Lengths of intestine and the tech-priest's inner workings spilled from the mess of his abdomen-stump.

'Halt,' the magos said, bringing the servitors to a stop. 'Status?'

'Compromised,' the medicae servitor told him in monotone. 'Critical. Demonstrated no life signs or data-feeds. Invasive interventions stabilised core and cogitae. Organic systems either dead or dying. Survival unlikely.'

What blood and oil remained in the priest's body was leaking out onto the stretcher. His augmented biology was still partially functioning, although he was technically not alive and in machine system shock. His hands reached out for things that were not there and nonsense fell from his lips like a stream of dribble.

'You know this priest?' Van Auken asked.

'Yes,' Urquidex informed him. 'The Omnissiah favoured him with my specialism: his name is Laurentis, Phaeton Laurentis. He was assigned to the original expedition.'

'Laurentis...'

'He did some good work in isolation, while attached to the Imperial Fists. He gathered some valuable data, made some useful observations.'

'His observations were not so useful to the Fabricator

General,' Van Auken said, 'when he transmitted them to Terra.'

'Like many of our calling,' Urquidex said, 'Phaeton Laurentis was not taken into the Fabricator General's confidence regarding the alien invader. He knew no more than the Guard officers and Adeptus Astartes besieged with him. We can hardly blame him for serving the cohort to which he had been assigned. And like I said, some of his work was very good, bearing in mind what little he had to work with.'

Van Auken was unconvinced. 'Take him to my shuttle,' the artisan commanded the servitors. 'He will repair to the ship for censure and redesignation of service.'

'Scrubbing him seems a waste,' Urquidex offered. 'He might have more information than was transmitted.' Van Auken considered the idea. 'Gathered between transmission and defeat.'

'It is undeniably true that such information would be useful,' Van Auken admitted. 'Inform the magi physic and artisans cybernetica that this priest is to be stabilised and readied for downstreaming and debriefing,' he told the servitors, before sending them off to his shuttle.

Van Auken turned, but Urquidex had already started the descent down into the excavated pit. There they found an infirmechanic standing among three waxy cocoons, taking readings. Humanoid in shape, the large cocoons appeared like the mummified ancients of some archaeological find. Instead of being wrapped in cloth, the three figures had secreted a kind of mucus-like residue that formed a thin, protective layer about their bodies. Through the membranous surface, the two priests could see the horror of mangled bodies: butchered torsos, missing limbs and scraps of ceramite plate. A yellow pauldron was visible through the stretched surface of one cocoon. The markings were clear even through the membrane: a black gauntlet, clutched into a defiant fist.

'They must have been buried in the gravitic upheaval,' the artisan trajectorae said. 'With the priest... Magos?'

'Aye,' Urquidex agreed, his telescopic eyes whirring in for a closer look. 'These are Adeptus Astartes genetic adaptations. A form of suspended animation, allowing them to survive all but the most mortal of wounds. The coating is an extreme form of protective secretion, airtight and temperature resistant. It is a wonder of genetic engineering.'

The magos biologis examined the infirmechanic's readings.

'Will they survive?' Van Auken asked him.

'Possibly.'

'Fascinating.'

'Their wounds are grievous and their life signs are practically non-existent.'

'Like the priest, they have first-hand knowledge of the enemy's tactical capabilities,' the artisan-primus said. 'You said it yourself. Better data than could be gathered by a thousand butchered drones.'

'Agreed,' Urquidex said. 'But I want you to know that if we break their suspension and revive them, we might not be able to save them from their injuries.'

'Their testimony is too important,' Van Auken said. 'It is required for the data packet.'

'The Adeptus Astartes – a successor Chapter – would have the specialist knowledge to...'

'We don't answer to the Adeptus Astartes,' Van Auken said. 'We answer to the Fabricator General.'

'These might be all that is left of the Imperial Fists.'

'Have them transported with the priest to the laboratorium aboard the *Subservius*,' Van Auken ordered. 'Begin suspension-interruption there.'

'You will take responsibility?'

'I will.'

ELEVEN

Terra – the Imperial Palace

The Senatorum Imperialis was in full session. It was an incredible sight. For Drakan Vangorich, it was a sight of byzantine bureaucracy and tedium. He had a thousand different ways to assemble relevant intelligence from such bloated, officious gatherings without actually having to attend them. He thought it unwise to miss too many meetings, however. Some personages were inevitably conspicuous by their absence. When the Grand Master of Assassins fails to make an appearance at such assemblies, the pervading boredom inflicted upon attendees prompts people to wonder where such a lord might be and what he might be doing. Wondering was not to be encouraged in the powerful and mighty. Wondering could get people killed.

No longer, though, was Vangorich a member of the High Twelve. Those dignitaries took their thrones on a central dais that turned almost imperceptibly, commanding a slowly revolving view of the stadium-seats, petitioners and functionaries. Below them, the Great Chamber was bustling with robed minor officials, their aides and advisors. Vangorich was not considered one of these minor officials by any means, but he did have to part a sea of the favour-curriers in order to pass long-deferred water. The path between his own allotted throne at the foot of Dorn's mighty statue and the ablutorials passed through the dour throngs of prefectii and consularies. Many lords of the Grand Master's office and station took the upper galleries to avoid such inconvenience. The paths to the private suites of specific influentials and the ablutorials were stalked by adepts, officials and officers waiting for *just a moment* of a High Lord's time or the slate-signature it might take to get rid of them swiftly. Some legistrae and ministrators had waited weeks, sometimes months, for a particular lord or significant to pass water. If it wasn't for the politics and the problems solved by such men over the fonts in the vestablutae antehalls, opportunistic encounters would have been an even rarer occurrence.

These were not considerations for Drakan Vangorich. The Grand Master cut through the clusters of officials like a dark knife. Few people on the Senatorum floor wanted to talk to an Assassin or be seen to talk to one. This suited Vangorich perfectly, and was why it surprised the Grand Master all the more when he was accosted.

'Master Vangorich,' a hooded aide said. 'A word with you, sir.'

Vangorich slowed and turned. A frown, the result of simultaneous curiosity and annoyance, sat on his face. He said nothing. The aide was dressed in drab, dark robes but carried herself with the confidence of one who knew she was addressing the deadliest man in the room, and didn't care. She was tall. The depths of her hood seemed to hide some kind of extravagant hair arrangement, as well as her face. Above the glint of dark intelligence in her eyes, a third optic – implanted in her brow and glowing a cold blue – created a triangular constellation in the shadows.

'So you're Kalthro's replacement,' Vangorich said, before turning his back on the Inquisitorial agent and setting off once again across the crowded Senatorum floor. The hooded operative's strides brought her alongside him only a moment later. 'Shame about Kalthro,' Vangorich said. 'I enjoyed our little games.'

'There will be no games to be had with me, my lord.'

'Nonsense,' the Assassin told her. 'We're just getting started. What's your name?'

'You do not need my name.'

'Nonetheless, I want it,' Vangorich said as they weaved through the officious masses. It seemed that Wienand's new bodyguard was no less secretive than her mistress. 'Is there not enough tedium in this chamber for you already? It will take nothing to learn it by other means.'

'And yet you don't already have it,' the woman said. 'Disappointing, Grand Master.'

'So you're their best?' Vangorich prodded, not rising to the taunt. 'After Kalthro, of course. What am I supposed to tell my best? Should I be warning them to look for you behind them?'

'That's what you're going to have to tell Esad Wire, formerly of Monitor Station KVF, Division 134, Sub 12.'

Vangorich narrowed his eyes. 'Nobody serves me under

that name,' he said. It was the truth, as far as it went. Wire's operative name was Beast.

'Call him what you like,' the woman said, 'but keep him off my cloak tails.'

'May I remind you that your predecessor got himself killed tailing my people, not the other way around,' Vangorich pointed out.

'My lady wishes to avoid further entanglements between our organisations,' the woman said.

'Understandable,' the Assassin said, 'considering the result of our last misunderstanding.'

'Lady Wienand considers it just that: a misunderstanding. There will be no retaliatory action. In fact, she appreciates your attempts to be of service during these difficult times. It is my impression that she even likes you, my lord – though for the Imperium, I cannot think why.'

'Is there a point to this?'

'She also implores you not to meddle further in these affairs. The Inquisition, in its investigatory capacity, will interrogate the present problems and take appropriate action. Protecting the Imperium from enemies within and without was the purpose for which the Inquisition was created. Lady Wienand urges you to honour this and restrict yourself and your agents to the parameters of your officio's own remit.'

'Do not lecture me on parameters and remits,' Vangorich bit back as he parted a throng of petitioners mobbing the Navigators' Paternoval Emissary. 'The Inquisition and its ill-recommended allies have denied the Senatorum intelligence essential to the Imperium's security. Billions have suffered for these machinations. Scores of worlds have been lost to an alien enemy, the existence and threat of which the Inquisition has kept hidden from the Imperium.'

'My lady apologises for not taking you into her confidences, my lord,' the Inquisitorial agent said. 'She sees now that you would and still could be a valued partner in our endeavours.'

'Yet her apologies fall from your lips?' Vangorich snapped.

The Inquisitorial agent gestured to the dais of thrones at the centre of the Great Chamber, one of which Inquisitorial Representative Wienand was occupying.

'She regrets that she is otherwise engaged, my lord,' the woman said. 'However, as a sign of good faith she has authorised me to share with you intelligence she knows you not to have.'

Vangorich gave the hooded operative the hardness of his eyes.

'Lady Wienand knows that the fleet movements that the Lord High Admiral announced today were procured by your good self through Ecclesiarch Mesring,' she went on. Still, Vangorich gave her nothing. 'As a courtesy, she wishes you to know that her eyes and ears within Navy command are aware of the full scope of the Lord High Admiral's manoeuvres.'

'And?' Vangorich said.

'Lansung will not redeploy his fleets,' the operative warned.

'The Lord High Admiral just announced, with Master Udo at his side, that he was recalling the border fleets,' Vangorich said, taking a chalice of fortified wine from a passing servitor-servant. His nostrils flared for a moment as he raised the wine to his lips, testing for potential toxins out of long-ingrained habit, before he drank it down and handed the empty vessel to another ceremonially-dressed vat-slave.

'Recalled, yes,' she said. 'Redeployed, no. Lansung is amassing an armada in the Glaucasian Gulf, off Lepidus Prime. There will be no deployment of Abel Verreault's Astra Militarum. The Ecclesiarch will honour his promise to you and declare a War of Faith.' The operative gestured once more to the High Twelve on their thrones. 'Just as soon as Lord Udo has completed his endless commendations of the Lord Admiral's foresight and decisive action. But with the Navy at void-anchorage in Glaucasia and the Chartist Captains pricing all but the wealthiest of the Ecclesiarch's crusaders out of passage across the rimward sectors, Mesring's war of faith is no more than a faithless war of words.'

'Why are you telling me this?' Vangorich said, his voice tight with anger.

'Lady Wienand wants your faith,' the agent said. 'The threat these dangers pose to the Imperium is beyond your meddlings and the operational scope of the Officio Assassinorum. Allow the Inquisition to fulfil its purpose. Stop creating ripples in the water. Even the best-intentioned actions could compromise our efforts. Trust in our determinations. Our organisation is young but able and best suited to meet this threat in its myriad forms. Leave us to our calling.'

'And if I don't?'

'If you are not part of the solution,' the operative said,

'and have no illusions, Grand Master, you are not, then you become part of the problem.'

Vangorich abruptly turned on the agent. A flash of alarm showed in her poise, though she tried to conceal it, and he felt a certain satisfaction at that. 'It seems appropriate that you should threaten me here, on the chamber floor of the Senatorum Imperialis,' he said, the coolness of his words at stark odds with the suddenness of his movements. 'You see, when the Emperor first envisaged the sprawling bureaucracy of such an organisation, many decried the fault in its design: the difficulty in harnessing the trust and concordance of so many factions and parties of interest. What they failed to appreciate was that the Emperor never wanted me to trust you. He never wanted you to trust me. That's the damnable beauty of it all. Our divisions and contrary motives are the checks and balances that such a large and powerful empire requires to keep it on course.

'We do face a crisis, that is true. I do believe that the Inquisition has an important role to play in its resolution. But the Inquistion – young, eager and growing in influence – will not use this crisis to grab the power your organisation craves'; for it craves it no less than the ancient offices and institutions already serving their self-interest. Your allies, through their action or omission of action, are endangering Imperial worlds. You will check their ambitions or you will force me to check them for you. In turn, I will be your check, your balance. For the good of the Imperium, the Officio Assassinorum will carry out one of the duties for which it was created and for which it is expertly suited – keeping the rest of the officios honest. Now,' Vangorich said, turning and heading for the ablutorials. 'Please excuse me. The wine, you see. It goes straight through me.'

As the Assassin walked through the gaggles of sycophants, towards the antehalls, he stopped a passing servitor-servant and took the final chalice of fortified wine from its silver tray. As he put the rim of the cup to his lips and drank, he watched the servitor mindlessly hold the polished platter at its side – as Vangorich had noticed the chamber drones do many times before. In the mirrored surface of the tray, the Grand Master saw the Inquisitorial agent watching his exit and a second figure, similarly robed and hooded, join her.

Vangorich studied the interloper's height and build: her slenderness and upright carriage obvious and her step light, even in the heavy robes. He had spent time studying that figure before for knowledge of her weight, balance, ambidexterity and reflexes; all he would need to know to get past her practiced defences and kill her with his bare hands. As she turned and the light picked out the sharpness of her cheekbones, Vangorich knew that he was looking at Inquisitorial Representative Wienand. The real Wienand: ghosting the chamber floor as a busy-body official, while some surgically-crafted double occupied her throne at the centre of the Great Chamber.

Vangorich watched her lips. He read their motions; the way they formed about words for which she had clear distaste. The pair studied him, little knowing that he was studying them right back. He watched Wienand's agent give the briefest of reports.

'Unfortunate,' he read from the light catching Wienand's lips.

'For you, my lady,' Vangorich said to himself, 'if you don't heed my warning.'

As Wienand and her bodyguard melted into the crowd, Vangorich gave the servitor-servant back the empty chalice. The withered thing replaced it on the silver tray and walked off, its service done. Passing the politics and double-dealing of the vestablutae fonts, Vangorich entered his reserved ablutory. Even the restrooms of the Imperial Palace had a grandness about their architecture and ornate fittings.

'Wait outside,' Vangorich commanded upon entrance, prompting a brass-masked servitor who performed the function of attendant to leave the small chamber. His privacy thus assured, the Assassin produced a vox-bead from his robes and slotted it into his ear.

'Beast...'

'Sir?'

'Mesring's found a way to screw us without screwing us,' Vangorich said.

'He told the Lord High Admiral.'

'The border fleets are being recalled but not redeployed,' the Grand Master spat. 'He's forming an armada.'

'A grand gesture,' Esad Wire voxed back. 'He can play galactic hero without risking a single vessel.'

'Or his influence in the Senatorum,' Vangorich said.

'Do you want me to withhold the antidote?' Esad Wire put to the Grand Master. Vangorich considered.

'He delivered half a solution,' he voxed to Beast. 'Issue him with the same. Have the antidote solution delivered at half concentration. Something to keep his Grace alive but still useful to us.'

'Consider it done.'

'Beast.'

'Yes, sir.'

'Meet me at Mount Vengeance.'

'Yes, my lord.'

'It's time we got to work.'

TWELVE

Aspiria System – Mandeville point

The void, usually so black and empty, was crowded with cataclysm. Colossal fragments of planetary rock tumbled through the darkness, smashing into and through one another. Shard storms of hull-punching regolith blossomed from such collisions, showering the tightening spaces between the gargantuan chunks of shattered planetoids with death. This was the edge of the Aspiria System, for Aspiria was no more.

An astrotelepathic distress call had drawn Marshal Bohemond's small crusader fleet to Aspira from the Vulpius region. The Black Templars' Vulpius Crusade had been in the Weald Worlds as part of a purgation action against the Noulia. The Adeptus Astartes had been the punch needed to break the xenos and had acted in support of a flotilla of Imperial Navy vessels under Commodore DePrasse, whose orbital bombardments had failed to obliterate the Noulia from the surface of the wooded, backwater moons.

Aspiria had been a large Imperial mining world that

dominated the system. Now, in its place, sat the ugly attack moon of which the astrotelepathic distress call had warned. The abominable thing bristled with gargantuan weaponry and fluxed with field shielding that routinely seemed to short and crackle away before returning with a blinding flash. Part of the monstrous moon was missing – perhaps the victim of a former planetary collision or malfunctioning weapon. In its place was a ramshackle framework of rusted girders and scaffolding, revealing the horrors of the planetoid interior: fleet bays and an internal anchorage for a barbarian armada of greenskin cruisers, attack ships and scrap-clads. Tearing the mine-riddled Aspiria to rubble with its great gravitic weaponry, the attack moon – like a spider's nest disgorging its young – streamed gunships, capsules and rocks at the surviving worlds of the system. What the bombardment of planetary debris didn't destroy, the swarms of delivered greenskins swiftly decimated. By the time the combination Black Templar and Imperial Navy fleet arrived, there was nothing but the enemy left.

Marshal Bohemond's gauntlets dug into the arms of his pulpit throne. It was not fear or concern for his safety that prompted his tightening grip, despite the tremors that felt their way through the battle-barge's superstructure and the command deck. It was anger. It was hatred. As the Black Templars battle-barge *Abhorrence* banked as sharply as its blunt prow and length would allow, a gargantuan piece of Aspiria tumbled by. Castellan Clermont, the battle-barge's commanding officer, had ordered the evasive manoeuvre. Never one to miss an opportunity to smite the xenos enemy, Clermont bawled at the bondsmen on the bridge to smash the battle-barge straight through a ragged vanguard line of ork ram ships and boarding hulks. Bohemond had allowed himself a moment of satisfaction with the castellan's strategy, imagining the xenos' surprise at the vessel they were intending to ram turning and crashing clean back through them. As the *Abhorrence* banked about the obstacle, however, with greenskin junkers detonating against the battle-barge's void shields, the bridge lancet screen revealed the xenos attack moon. Bohemond felt bile climb the back of his throat. Like the tug of tiny threads in the muscles of his face, his mouth formed an involuntary snarl.

Bohemond had fought the greenskins many times before. Gililaq 3-16. Horner's World. Gamma Phorsk. Draakoria. It had been on Draakoria that a feral greenskin shaman had taken his eye. With its unnatural powers the creature had set everything around it alight, but Bohemond had strode through the strange flame using his hatred of the thing as his compass. The marshal had slain its chieftain and thousands of its depraved tribe-kin, and had promised himself that the witch would suffer the same fate. With his blade encrusted with greenskin gore, the marshal had charged through the inferno.

The wyrd-creature had saved a little of itself for the encounter, however, and had called upon its sorcery to bathe Bohemond in a blazing stream so powerful and intense that it all but scorched the ceramite plate from his body. Dropping his sword and holding an outstretched gauntlet before his disintegrating helm, Bohemond had managed to save an eye and part of his face. With much of his roasted armour falling from his burnt flesh in a cloud

of cinders and his hair still alight, the Black Templar had stomped through his agony and on towards the despised alien. Grabbing the spent monster, he had beaten the greenskin to death with his sizzling fists.

As he beheld the attack moon with his one good eye, Bohemond felt the soul-scalding hatred he had felt for the green plague of Draakoria resurface. He knew he was in the presence of something alien, unnatural and abominable. Something well-deserving of its end. Deserving of Dorn's cold wrath and the instruments of his zealous fury: the Black Templars.

As the *Abhorrence* resumed its course and the planetary decimation of the Aspiria mining world began to clear, the derelict madness of the greenskin fleet came into focus. Between the battle-barge and the ork attack moon lay a blizzard of vagabond vessels. Jury-rigged derelicts. Drifting cannon-platforms. Rocketing voidscrap. Ungainly experiments in sub-light engineering and death. Bohemond's teeth gleamed from within his widening snarl. The marshal would only be at peace standing in his battleplate beneath the surface of the moon, slaughtering its denizens. Between him and that purity of purpose lay a small armada of inconvenience.

'Castellan,' the Marshal called. 'Order the *Umbra* to pull back.' Bohemond had noticed that the strike cruiser had drawn ahead of the *Abhorrence.*

'Commander Godwin wants to be let off the leash,' Clermont observed.

'I sympathise,' Bohemond growled. 'You can tell him that Rogal Dorn himself blesses this action.' Bohemond turned in his pulpit throne and looked up for confirmation at Chaplain Aldemar. The Chaplain didn't return his marshal's gaze. With his cenobyte slaves clutching Chapter relics about him and his face hidden behind the featureless faceplate of his Crusader helmet, Aldemar merely nodded slowly. '*Abhorrence*, however, has the honour of leading the charge,' Bohemond continued. 'Order *Sodalitas* and *Sword of Sigismund* to take station on our flanks. The *Ebon* and *Bona Fide* are to support the *Umbra* in protecting our ships on the approach. All vessels to fall behind the battle-barge and benefit from the protection of our forward shields. The enemy are many and will hit us hard, but we will endure. Like a bolt-round through their miserable scraps of armour, we will punch through their assemblage of hulks and junkers.'

As bridge serfs fell to relaying Bohemond's orders, Castellan Clermont asked, 'And what orders for Commodore DePrasse, marshal?'

'Tell the commodore to have his captains form a line of battle behind us,' Bohemond commanded. 'His ships may fire as they bear. We shall take them through the greenskin armada, where we will need the big guns of his capital ships to support the *Abhorrence* in cracking that abominate moon open. Meanwhile, the Black Templars shall bring havoc to the xenos wretches hiding within.'

'Relaying now, marshal,' Clermont said.

'Frater Astrotechnicus,' Bohemond called. Techmarine Kant was standing amongst a nest of bondsmen and bridge servitors, monitoring the enginarium rune banks.

'Yes, marshal,' Kant replied without moving his stapled

Bohemond jabbed a vox-stub in the arm of his pulpit-throne with a ceramite digit. 'Captain Ulbricht, this is the marshal. You are authorised to board Thunderhawks and assault ships in preparation for void insertion. I will join you on the final approach.'

'I would expect nothing less, marshal,' Ulbricht voxed back from the launch bays. 'As the xenos will recieve nothing less than annihilation, ardent and absolute.'

'Very good, captain,' Bohemond said. 'Stand by for the order to launch. Accelerate to ramming speed,' the marshal added to his bridge crew as the *Abhorrence* plunged towards the enemy ship swarm. Both Space Marine and bondsman felt the sudden change in velocity shudder through the decking as the battle-barge's mighty drives pushed them onwards into the oncoming greenskin barrage.

'Crusader cruisers and frigates accelerating in line with new speed and heading,' a bridge bondsman announced.

'Marshal,' Clermont called. 'We appear to have a problem.'

'Report.'

'We've lost vox-contact with the commodore's flagship.'

'Lost contact?' Bohemond rumbled. 'Is the *Magnificat* under attack?'

'The battleship is yet to engage,' Clermont said.

'Kant?'

'Nothing on augurstream or binary frequencies,' the

Techmarine reported with metallic reverb. 'The Navy vessels are slowing, marshal.'

'The *Preservatorio*? The *Falchiax*? The *Thunderfall*?'

'Static, my lord,' the castellan said.

'Try the destroyers and the heavy escorts,' the marshal barked. 'What the hell is he doing?'

'Only the cruiser *Aquillon* is keeping pace with our approach, marshal,' Clermont reported after failing to contact the smaller commands. 'Captain Grenfell, my lord.'

'Kant – could this be the xenos? Their technology overwhelming our communications?'

'Arrays and transmitters are returning both trace waves and background radiation,' the Techmarine returned. 'Vox-transmissions between the battle-barge and crusader vessels are unaffected.'

'My lord.' The barbican bondsman who had been stationed by the bridge doors presented himself, pulling back his hood.

'What is it?'

'I realise that it's irregular, marshal,' the bondsman said, 'but the battle-barge astropath craves a moment of your time. He asks for permission to enter the command deck.'

'Does he not know we are about to enter into battle?' Bohemond seethed. The Black Templar was furious enough with Commodore DePrasse. A detested audience with one of the only psykerbreeds allowed on board the ship would probably drive the marshal over the edge.

'I would ordinarily forbid it, my lord,' the bondsman said, not wishing to attract the Marshal's ire. 'But he insisted it was important. Something about the communications issue.'

Bohemond looked from the bondsman to Clermont, then from the castellan to Chaplain Aldemar. The Chaplain nodded slowly and solemnly.

'Admit him,' the marshal said.

'Master Izericor,' the barbican bondsman announced.

Izericor shuffled onto the bridge, his staff tapping before him across the unfamiliar command deck. He bowed and drew back his hood. Blinders, like those found on livestock, partially hid the ragged holes where the astropath's eyes used to be.

'You have intelligence for me?' Bohemond snarled.

'I have just intercepted a message, my lord,' Izericor said with deferent enthusiasm. 'A communiqué of such import that I risk your displeasure, marshal.'

'Speak,' Bohemond said with difficulty. 'What know you of our communication difficulties?'

'Commodore DePrasse has just received new orders from Terra, my lord,' the psyker said. 'Commandments that supersede your own.'

'What new orders?' Castellan Clermont demanded.

'The commodore is ordered to take his flotilla to a Navy rendezvous point in the Glaucasian Gulf, as soon as possible.'

'Whose authority is carried by this communiqué?' Bohemond asked.

'The message bears the telesignature of Teegas Urelia, astrotelepath to Lord High Admiral Lansung himself.'

'They're playing for time,' Clermont said. 'They don't know what to do for the best: disobey an order or offend the Adeptus Astartes.'

Marshal Bohemond suddenly took to his feet, prompting even the blind Izericor to step back.

'Send a telepathic communiqué to the chief astropath aboard the *Magnificat*,' Bohemond said, his voice low and furious. 'Tell him that I want an explanation from his master presently or I am coming over to the flagship myself.'

'Marshal...' the castellan started.

'Do it!' Bohemond bellowed, causing the astropath to jump.

'As you command,' Izericor replied.

'The enemy lines,' Techmarine Kant announced. 'Brace for impact.'

While the bondsmen and servitors reached out for handles and restraints, the Black Templars rode out the tremor, the magnetic soles of their boots keeping them in place. The forward void shields flashed and flared with a storm of impacts. First came a short range wave of torpedoes, kamikaze bombcraft and macrocannon blasts. This onslaught was followed by beak-prowed gunships and ramming hulks that would have delivered their brute cargoes of boarding orks if they hadn't detonated against the intensity of the battle-barge's void shields. As the *Abhorrence* ploughed on through the crude belligerence of greenskin engineering and weaponry, the aggression and monstrous bulk of the opposing vessels increased, with cruisers and gun-hulks manoeuvring into the battle-barge's irresistible path.

'Marshal,' Clermont called as an obscenity masquerading as a battlecruiser drifted a rusted broadside before the Black Templars battle-barge. Bohemond nodded.

'Explain it to these savages,' the Marshal sneered.

Clermont jabbed his gauntlet at several bridge bondsmen. 'Ready bombardment cannon.'

'Weapon standing by, castellan.'

'Fire!'

The battle-barge bucked as its dorsal cannon fired, sending a magma-bomb warhead streaking ahead of the prow. As it struck the ork battlecruiser, a searing explosion rippled through the reinforced scrap of the derelict's side. The mountain of salvage broke away in two sections, between which the *Abhorrence* charged on.

'Is it done?' Bohemond demanded.

'It is, my lord,' the battle-barge's astropath answered.

Moments passed. Wreckage drifted clear of the lancet screens. Explosions flashed and rumbled before the void shields. Greenskin gunships drew in with their puncture-prows and grapnels, like predators of the deep.

'Vox-transmission from the *Magnificat*, marshal,' a bondsmen broke the silence on the bridge. 'Flag Lieutenant Esterre.'

Clermont saw the flutter of cold fury pass across his marshal's grizzled features.

'Put the flag lieutenant on the loudhailer,' Bohemond commanded.

After a brief burst of static, a patrician voice cut across the command deck.

'Am I addressing Marshal Bohemond?'

'The question, flag lieutenant,' Bohemond rumbled, 'is why on Terra aren't I addressing your commodore?'

'Commodore DePrasse is currently indisposed, marshal,' the flag lieutenant explained with silky authority. 'Please accept his humble apologies.'

'I am waging war against the xenos as we speak,' Bohemond told him, 'yet I am still in contact with force contingents – as protocols dictate.'

'Again, marshal: please accept my apologies.'

'Damnation take your apologies,' Bohemond boomed. 'You think it prudent to lie to an Adeptus Astartes?'

The vox-stream went silent. There was no protocol for this. 'This is the heat of battle, lieutenant. We do not have time for anything other than the truth: cold and swift. Think before you answer. I hold all of the Emperor's subjects accountable for their actions – and inaction. Have no doubt, for the Black Templars, the latter is the graver offence.'

Lieutenant Esterre seemed to take a moment. Perhaps he was considering his future in the Imperial Navy. Perhaps he was simply considering his future. Perhaps he was conferring with a peer or superior.

'We have received a recall, Marshall,' Esterre told him, the truth uneasy on his lips. 'The Lord High Admiral himself requires the commodore and his flotilla at a rendezvous above Lepidus Prime. We have no choice: it's a vermillion-level order.'

'And I'm not suggesting you don't follow it, lieutenant,' Bohemond said. 'Attend your rendezvous, haul off to Lepidus Prime – just after the completion of this action. When victory is in our grasp and the enemy threat eradicated.'

Static. Silence.

'Lieutenant, this is Castellan Clermont. We need *Magnificat*'s heavy guns. We need the *Preservatorio* and *Falchiax.* We need the *Thunderfall*'s lances. We cannot crack the xenos attack moon without them. We can't do it.'

'My lords,' Flag Lieutenant Esterre came back, 'I suspect there is little that the Adeptus Astartes cannot do.'

'Then you know how much it pains a son of Dorn to admit as much,' Clermont retorted. 'Your vermillion-level order no doubt concerns manoeuvres reacting to this new enemy threat.'

'The threat is here, Esterre,' Bohemond said. 'Why pull corewards when we can end these mongrelbreeds here on the segmentum rim?'

'I'm sorry, marshal,' Esterre said finally. 'I really am. We all have our orders. Commodore DePrasse intends to follow his. *Magnificat* out.'

'Esterre...' Marshall Bohemond roared. His anger echoed about the cavernous command deck.

'He's gone,' a bondsman informed him. 'Vox-link broken from their end. The *Magnificat* is hauling off.'

'Open channel,' Clermont ordered. 'All frequencies. Captains and commanders: this is the battle-barge *Abhorrence* requesting fire support, coordinates three, fifty-six, fifty-two. We are under attack. We are invoking section four-two-seven of the Vortangelo-Heidrich Proclamation signed by Marshal Grigchter and Grand Admiral Hadrian Okes-Martin during the Auriga Wars. This is *Abhorrence*, requesting fire support.'

Clermont waited. About the battle-barge, turrets cut through boarding rocks and breaching capsules. Broadsides crashed through terror ships and gun-hulks. A sea of wreckage and void mines tested the battle-barge's forward shields, with the *Abhorrence*'s prow forced to crash through the crowded chaos.

'*Preservatorio*, hauling off, sir,' a bondsman announced. '*Thunderfall*, hauling off. *Falchiax*, hauling off...'

Clermont looked to his marshal. Bohemond had slammed his armoured form back into his pulpit-throne.

'Marshal,' the castellan said. 'Without the *Magnificat* or the commodore's cruisers, we cannot hope to damage the xenos abomination.'

'*Oligarch Constantius*, hauling off,' the bondsman droned. '*Ministering Angel*, hauling off. *Morning Star*, hauling off. *Tiberius Rex*, hauling off.'

'Marshal...'

'Who's still with us?' Bohemond murmured.

'Marshal...'

'With which vessels do we still keep attendance, castellan?' the marshal insisted.

After conferring with the bridge bondsman, Clermont said: 'The *Aquillon* – Dictator-class cruiser, Captain Grenfell. The *Firebrand* – Lancet-class corvette, Commander Ulanti. Neither vessel fields lance decks.'

Bohemond clasped the arms of his throne with both gauntlets. The alloy of the pulpit-seat creaked beneath the pressure. His good eye was set in an unswerving gaze on the enemy attack moon. The marshal's face was bathed in red as emergency lamps and alarms erupted across the command deck.

'Kant?' Castellan Clermont called, but before the Techmarine could confirm the threat, several greenskin vessels gunning down on the battle-barge formed a train of explosions. One after another, drawing closer and closer to the *Abhorrence*, the junkers detonated.

The train of destruction ended with the *Sodalitas*. One moment the the strike cruiser was there. The next it had been replaced by a streaking implosion of ignited fuel and hallowed wreckage. Its armoured prow and thoraxial gun decks had been smashed straight back through its engine columns and immaterial drives, as though an invisible fist had crashed through the vessel. No one on the *Abhorrence* had seen the atrocity, but every member of the battle-barge's crew felt the swell of the explosion ring through the decks.

'Starboard evasive!' Clermont called. The battle-barge lurched and banked sharply.

'Commander Klein of the *Bona Fide* reports the *Sodalitas* destroyed,' a bondsman called from where he was clinging to his rune bank.

'Confirmed,' the castellan reported. 'Strike cruiser *Sodalitas* is lost. Forty-one battle-brothers and two hundred and sixteen bonded crew dead, marshal.'

The report struck Bohemond like a physical blow. He turned to Chaplain Aldemar. The Chaplain said nothing. He sank slowly to his armoured knees on the command deck and began his murmured obsequies and the sacraments of the fallen.

'Kant, I need that–' Clermont began.

'Some kind of gravitic weapon,' Kant called back. 'Vectored and directional. The planet-smasher the attack moon must have used on Aspiria.'

'Marshal?'

'Have all Chapter vessels and Navy attendants form up behind the battle-barge,' Bohemond ordered.

'Sir, we are outnumbered–'

'And what means that to the Black Templars?'

'The enemy has the advantage,' the castellan attempted to continue.

'You have just summarised the beginning of every worthy battle in which the Black Templars have fought,' Marshal Bohemond declared proudly.

'Every worthy battle that Black Templars survived, marshal,' Clermont replied. 'But this will see us all dead before we can scratch them.'

'Steel yourself, brother,' Bohemond said. 'These thoughts proceed from some cowardly corner of your soul.'

'No such place exists, my lord.'

'Well it must, Castellan Clermont,' Bohemond roared back, 'for I hear the suggestion of a retreat in your guarded advisements.'

'Brothers!' Techmarine Kant called, but he wasn't calling for reconciliation. A chain of explosions were ripping through the void. Greenskin salvage-clads and gun-hulks formed a thunderbolt of sequential detonations, terminating in an assault on the Black Templars battle-barge. Bohemond was thrown from his pulpit-throne and Chaplain Aldemar from his devotions. Rune banks, augur stations and cogitae spat sparks and crackled with overloaded energy. Two Chapter bondsmen lay dead, while injuries and malfunctions had been inflicted upon a number of servitors and bridge crew. Smoke soaked up the bloody menace of the emergency lamps and klaxons screeched their urgency.

The *Abhorrence* had taken a direct hit from the attack moon's gravitic planet-smasher on its intensified forward void shields. Proximity warnings joined the din of alarms on the bridge. Falling away from its surging course into a drunken drift, the battle-barge almost collided with the *Sword of Sigismund*.

'Damage report,' Clermont managed, clawing himself up a console station and back to his feet. A ragged gash ran parallel to the service studs stamped into his forehead. Kant, with his bionic adaptations and extra weight, had been the only unsecured member of the bridge crew not to end up on the deck.

'Datastreams struggling to carry reports and diagnostics,' Kant said. 'So far I have some structural damage and electrical fires.'

Clermont moved between the bondsmen and servitors, who had fortunately been buckled into the station-seats. He cast his eyes across their flashing runescreens.

'Seventeen fatalities reported amongst the crew,' the castellan said, 'mainly impact damage. No battle-brothers. Captain Ulbricht reports the Thunderhawks *Smite* and *Purgator's Dawn* damaged and battle-unworthy.'

'Void shields are down to twenty-two per cent nominal capacity,' Kant said.

'Brother,' Clermont urged, turning to Bohemond.

'The *Abhorrence* cannot withstand another hit like that,' Kant added grimly.

'Marshal,' the castellan said, marching forwards. 'We must withdraw.'

Bohemond was back on his feet. Despite having fallen, his gaze had barely left the hated attack moon.

'It is cowardice...' Bohemond hissed through his teeth.

'No more, my lord,' Clermont assured him, 'than when I defer battle to adorn myself with plate and recover my blade and bolter.'

Bohemond looked at his castellan.

'These beasts will keep,' Clermont told his marshal. 'We shall return, as we have before, in greater number – in greater fervour – with the tools to finish this job. Aspiria is lost. Since translating in-system, Master Izericor has received numerous mortis-cries but also requests for aid.'

The astropath, toppled also, had somehow found his way back to his sandalled feet and his staff. Noticing him, Bohemond's expression resumed its former hostility.

'It is true, marshal,' Izericor said. 'The hive-world of Undine is besieged – but then so are the hive-worlds of Plethrapolis and Macromunda. The Gormandi agri-worlds are under attack. The Mechanicus invoke ancient treaties and concords. They are losing the twin forge-worlds of Incus Maximal and Malleus Mundi to the invader.'

Clermont went to interrupt, but the astropath hadn't finished. 'The First Quashanid storm troop – the so-called Immortals – are holding the fortress-world of Promentor. The penal world of Turpista IV is also holding out longer than expected. Both have requested assistance. Both have proven that they would make excellent holdpoints. Your brethren of battle and blood, the Fists Exemplar, fight for their fortress-monastery and their world, Eidolica. The list goes on, my lord.'

Clermont and Bohemond locked gazes, Templar to Templar.

'The rimward sectors call for the Emperor's Angels,' the

castellan told his marshal. 'They call for the Black Templars. We have no world to defend. We have crusades. We have only wars and the worlds upon which we choose to wage them. The green plague is upon the segmentum. Isn't there enough of the invader to go around?'

Bohemond turned to the Chaplain, who was on his knees and at one with his devotions.

'Aldemar?'

The drone of cult litanies from within the Chaplain's helm came to a stop.

'Choose, brother,' Aldemar told him.

Bohemond of the Black Templars looked to his friend and castellan.

'Order the flotilla to break up,' the marshal commanded. 'Multiple targets will give individual vessels the best chance against that monstrous weapon.'

'Yes, Marshal.'

'All crusader contingents to rendezvous at the Mandeville point.'

'Yes, marshal.'

'All vessels, make preparations for immaterial translation.'

'Yes, marshal.'

'Do you have a destination in mind, sir?' Castellan Clermont asked.

'Yes,' Marshal Bohemond replied. 'I do.'

THIRTEEN

Ardamantua – orbital

The Adeptus Mechanicus survey brig *Subservius* drifted in orbit around Ardamantua, eventually becoming lost in the shadow of the *Amkulon*. The cruiser was a shattered wreck, a reminder of the power and ferocity visited upon Ardamantua by the xenos weapon. The gravitational disturbances about the planet continued to subside, but slowly. Although the *Amkulon* was useless for salvage – even the greenskins had left the radioactive wreck behind – it did provide the smaller survey brig with an anchor-point of stability, created by the natural gravity of the derelict cruiser's own tumbling form.

Magos Biologis Eldon Urquidex was thankful for the extra stability. His magi physic and artisans cybernetica needed all they could get to carry out the delicate procedures to which they had been committed for the last few hours. The medicae section of the laboratorium was crowded with surgeomats and servitors. On three surgical slabs lay the cocoons recovered from the Ardamantuan surface. The three Imperial Fists. The only surviving Adeptus

Astartes of a proud and decorated Chapter. The true sons of Dorn – now butchered, half-living remnants of suspended existence.

As the last line of defence that their superhuman bodies had to offer, Urquidex thought it unwise to have them cut them out of their membranous sheathing. Instead, he had his magi gathered about the huge bodies and operated on them within their protective cocoons. About the crowded slabs, with multiple procedures being conducted at the same time, Urquidex had summoned every adept on board the *Subservius* that might be able to offer their expertise. Scanners and field-auspexes monitored the Adeptus Astartes' life signs, calibrated specifically for their superhuman biology. Their genetic signatures confirmed what their scraps of decimated plate had already suggested – that they were indeed members of the Imperial Fists extermination force dispatched to Ardamantua to destroy the nest infestations of the Chrome vermin-species. Their life signs, however, were excruciatingly low and fading.

As Magos Urquidex and his team fought to save the Adeptus Astartes, with equipment and consultation exchanged across the bodies, Magos Phaeton Laurentis had been placed on a tracked stretcher-slab, positioned to one side of the surgical chamber. Medicae servitors had stabilised what was left of the tech-priest, while the chief artisan cybernetica had surgically truncated his lower torso and interfaced it for the bionic adaptations that would follow. With the Adeptus Astartes in such critical condition, there had been little time for more superficial repairs and diagnostics. Madness still poured continually from the priest's ruined lips and his spidery fingers still reached out for objects that were not there. Artisan-Primus Van Auken had ordered Laurentis' cogitae-core downstreamed for useful code and observational data.

Van Auken himself observed from an armourglass bubble-port in the thick laboratorium wall. This was habit. The facility was a maximum security laboratorium that up until this point had housed dissections on living or dead specimens of *Veridi giganticus*. Alpha Primus Orozko of the Epsil-XVIII Collatorax and a skitarii security detail stood with the artisan-primus. Van Auken knew he would be of little help actually in the chamber but wanted to remain in attendance to ensure that Eldon Urquidex followed his instructions regarding the remaining Imperial Fists to the letter. Meanwhile, Van Auken orchestrated the Adeptus Mechanicus survey team's extraction from the Ardamantuan surface and made final revisions to the data packet he intended to send to Mars.

The artisan trajectorae had insisted that Urquidex, as the only senior priest not to have completed his report, deliver his data. Van Auken was eager to leave Ardamantua and move the survey brig on to Macromunda, where the xenos invasion was still in its early stages. The data packet needed to be transmitted first and Van Auken felt that the results of the Adeptus Astartes' resurrection, and if possible their initial testimonies, should be included. Besides, Eldon Urquidex had insisted that the *Subservius* not be in transit and hold in as stable an orbit as possible while the hours of life-saving procedures were attempted.

It was not going well. Despite the best efforts of the priests, the Adeptus Astartes were fading away. Their injuries had been horrific testament to the Beast's savages and the brutality of greenskin weaponry. That the Emperor's Angels should be smashed and blasted thus was a reminder to all in the laboratorium that the greenskin invader was not to be underestimated.

For Van Auken, it was a reminder of a power and potency to be studied and harnessed. For if the greatest weapons of Terra's Emperor had failed – the gene-heirs of warriors who had fought the renegade Warmaster's forces on the walls of the Imperial Palace – then truly the capabilities of the savage enemy race warranted further study.

When the first of the Adeptus Astartes died, the laboratorium went into overdrive. As the life signs flatlined, priests and medicae servitors swarmed about the subject. Frantic magi were up to their elbows in gore. Metal receptacles clanged as slab servo-pincers extracted shards of frag and fat bullets, depositing them in rapidly filling scuttles. Surge-omats administered synthetic infusions and stimulants directly to the hearts. The second Space Marine swiftly followed his brother, splitting the magi and servitors between the hulking patients.

The laboratorium should have been clouded with regret and high emotion. The loss of any subject on the surgical slab would have prompted such reactions from common Imperial medics and planetary doctors. The significance of the event should have raised the emotional stakes higher. Before the priests' eyes and augmetics, the last of the honoured Imperial Fists Chapter were breathing their last. Bleeding their last. Feeling their last.

The laboratorium was crowded with priest-subjects of the Adeptus Mechanicus, however, for whom such emotions were meaningless. Their fight for life was a battle with the inevitability of ignorance. If the Adeptus Astartes died then opportunities would be missed, data would be incomplete and further researches impossible. The best the Omnissiah's servants could summon was the barest suggestion of professional remonstration. Even in failure, however, the Machine God's acolytes reasoned there were opportunities to learn and make improvements. Autopsies could still reveal secrets of value to the Grand Experiment.

With two of his patients falling victim to the wounds that they had suffered on Ardamantua, Magos Urquidex brought all of his assistants about the remaining subject. The laboratorium was a cacophony of offered opinions, binary cant, suggested surgeries, the whine of las-scalpels and auspectoria alarms. As the Adeptus Astartes' life signs faded, the frenetic activity intensified. The subject went into arrest. Tests became increasingly savage and invasive. Brutal cybernetic transplants were attempted. Blood fountained at the laboratorium ceiling.

'We're losing the subject,' a magos physic announced.

As the Space Marine's life signs evaporated and biological death was confirmed, the procedures doubled in their bloodthirsty desperation. By the time the priests and servo-cybernetica had finished with the Space Marine's engineered form, it looked like he had been turned inside out. Most of his organs were outside of his body and the protective cocoon was now a shredded and gore-soaked sheath.

'That's it,' Eldon Urquidex said finally. 'Summon the magi concisus: the holy work of the subjects' design and genetic workings should be honoured. Last rites should be issued before autopsy is conducted.'

Taking surgical towels from a servitor, Urquidex looked up through the armourglass of the observation bubble as he cleaned the worst of the gore from his hands and appendages. 'Record the time, date and location, accounting for galactic drift and chrono-dilation. Nobody will ever know, but we just slaughtered the last of the Imperial Fists on our surgical slab.'

'Again, magos,' Van Auken told him, 'you must learn to govern your sentimentality. Fellow magi and adepts. Your exemplary efforts have been noted in the mission log. You are dismissed.'

As the laboratorium emptied of Adeptus Mechanicus personnel, Urquidex and Van Auken continued to stare at one another.

'What did we learn?' the artisan trajectorae demanded.

Urquidex deposited his stained surgical towel in an incinerator chute. 'That the Adeptus Astartes' chemical therapies and implants were doing a better job of preserving the Imperial Fists than our surgeries, infusions and cybernetic transplants.'

'You think me wrong to insist on your efforts?'

'Absolutely,' Urquidex told him. 'And I would like my objection noted in the log.'

'Entered already,' Van Auken said. 'But I wonder, who are you more concerned for? The subject on the slab, or yourself and your failure to save him?'

'I'm sure that I don't comprehend your meaning, artisan-primus.'

'Let me put it another way,' Van Auken said. 'I think your sentimentality a falsehood. You suffer no less from the vagaries of pride than the rest of the priesthood. We are all judged by our work. You fear the Fabricator General's disappointment, no less than I. You don't want to be assigned to some Eastern Fringe dead-world research station for eternity, studying fossilised evidence of silica nematodes. The Omnissiah is willing to forgive failure, given that it is a step on the journey to success. Failing to embark on the journey in the first place is the sin of ignorance, and the Machine God and his servants are less willing to forgive you that.'

'I think you will find the Adeptus Astartes even less forgiving than that,' Urquidex said.

'Are you threatening me, magos?' Van Auken said coolly.

'Let's just hope that the Adeptus Astartes never have reason to visit the Eastern Fringe,' Urquidex said. 'Will there be anything else, artisan-primus?'

The priests stared at each other through the thick observation-port armourglass.

'What of the recovered magos?' Van Auken said finally.

'Magos Biologis Phaeton Laurentis is now the only official survivor of the Ardamantuan atrocity,' Urquidex said, turning to where the half-priest lay on his stretcher-slab.

He wasn't there.

Urquidex discovered that the magos biologis had reached down his stretcher-slab and unlocked the brake before hauling the tracked gurney across the laboratorium by heaving arm-over-arm on a line of cables and data-feeds.

His exhausting efforts had brought his stretcher-slab over to where the last Imperial Fist had been surgically butchered and had died. Urquidex and Van Auken watched as Laurentis – his ruined mouth continuing to babble trauma-induced nonsense – placed his hand on the Imperial Fist's yellow pauldron.

'It seems that sentimentality is a disease common to your specialism,' Van Auken accused. Urquidex ignored him and watched the magos biologis with fascination. Pushing himself off the pauldron, Laurentis snatched at the fibre cabling running between the Adeptus Astartes' body and the auspectoria banks. Moving his smashed, skeletal digits across the instrumentation, the tech-priest fell to adjusting calibrations and auspectra frequencies.

'Are you going to stand by and allow a delirious patient to disrupt the settings of your equipment, magos?' Van Auken said. 'He might be erasing precious data of the previous procedures.'

'The Third Law of Universal Variance,' Urquidex murmured.

'The Bystander Paradox?'

'Do not interfere,' Urquidex said.

Slamming his bloodied palm against a fat stud, Laurentis completed his reprogramming of the laboratorium equipment. The flatline feed and mortis-tone died abruptly. It was replaced with a distant, signature life sign. The very faintest beat of twin hearts.

'What is that?' Van Auken demanded.

Urquidex walked up to the instrumentation and placed a hand on the forehead of the butchered half-priest. His chest was rising and falling with exertion and his brow was moist. His babblings continued unabated. Looking closely at the field-auspex, he discovered that the magos had set it to a broad-range scan.

'It's a fourth life sign,' Urquidex informed him. 'Very weak. Buried below the others.' He began punching buttons and twisting dials on the rune bank. 'I'm rerouting this data to the bridge. Alpha primus, if you please.'

Through the armourglass bubble-port, Orozko was already on the observation deck vox-hailer. The feeble heartbeats continued. Nothing like the thunder they once must have been, but insistent nonetheless. Both Van Auken and Urquidex looked to the skitarii officer.

'Ship augur arrays have boosted and traced the signal,' the alpha primus said finally. 'The life sign is confirmed as Adeptus Astartes. It's coming from the wreck of the *Amkulon*.'

'Holy Mars,' Urquidex said. 'The radiation.'

'Artisan-primus,' Orozko said. 'Several members of your trajectorae team are on the bridge. They say that the signal betrays the trace power signature of recent trans-vectoring.'

'A teleportation homer?'

'Yes, artisan-primus.'

'Van Auken?' Urquidex called through the armourglass. 'How can we have only detected this now?'

'The gravitic disturbances inflicted on the system might have had an inhibiting effect on the teleportation technologies,' the artisan trajectorae hypothesised. 'With the removal of the affecting body – the xenos attack moon – the disturbance subsided and the vectoring achieved realisation.'

'Life signs are extremely weak,' Urquidex reported.

The artisan-primus nodded. 'Alpha primus – please select an extraction team from your men. The survivor must be recovered and removed from the toxic environment of the derelict.'

'Yes, artisan-primus.'

'Alpha primus,' Van Auken added, 'this is a mortis-mission. The skitarii returning from the *Amkulon* will be compromised and not expected to survive.'

'I shall send Vanguard units. They are already radiation-compromised,' Orozko replied dourly before leaving the observation deck.

When Van Auken turned back to the observation port he found Magos Urquidex standing at the armourglass.

'It seems that a trip to the Eastern Fringe is not required to achieve an audience with the Adeptus Astartes, after all,' Urquidex said.

'Keep this one alive,' Van Auken said coldly, 'and such a trip might not be necessary.' With that the artisan-primus departed the observation deck and left Magos Urquidex to his half-priest patient.

FOURTEEN

Undine – submerged

It was all but impossible to find a private space aboard the armed submersible *Tiamat*. Both space and privacy existed at a premium below the Undinian waves, and never more so than now, following the attack on Hive Pherusa. Commander Lux Allegra knew this better than most, but still managed to find a tiny maintenance alcove in the steam-swathed engineering compartment. A place for kneeling. For gritted teeth. For trembling hands. For tears that would not come.

General Phifer and Admiral Novakovic had ordered the planetary defence fleet to put in at Pherusa for supplies, munitions and manpower. The greenskin invasion force had yet to reach the mercantile hive and the city boasted an impressive harbour. While the freighters and troop carriers took on contingents of Undine Marineers and recruits, sky talons drifted fuel and munitions over to Novakovic's launch carriers and heavy monitors. By the time the skies darkened to the east, it was already too late. Without orbital augur arrays to warn the defence fleet, Phifer and Novakovic could have little idea what was coming. So much that they had witnessed of the greenskin invasion had been unprecedented. The attack on Pherusa Harbour was no different.

Blotting out the heavens ahead of the storm of raining crash-capsules and rocks was a greenskin wing comprising an assortment of fat aircraft, flying citadels and super-heavy bombers. The colossal junkers had monstrous bellies packed to the rivets with mega-bombs and weapons of mass destruction. Their thunderous engines barely kept the bombers in the air, while their wing expanses formed runways for smaller jets and kamikaze rockets. Their bulbous hulls swarmed with kopters and mounted accreted platforms for fat cannons, launchers and macrostubbers. The bomber wing's approach was slow and irresistible, eclipsing the sun and casting a great shadow across the ocean.

The admiral's Avenger formations were swallowed whole by the droning monster. The hive's turbo weaponry and the defence fleet's deck-mounted cannons punched holes in the swarm but could do nothing to stop the deluge of greenskin ordnance that dropped from the sky. Monitors and corvettes erupted in cloud-scraping fireballs. Multi-hulled launch carriers were blasted in two. Overcrowded transports went to the bottom of the anchorage, taking thousands of defence force guardsmen with them. Marineers. Mercenaries. Volunteers. Men and women who would have fought for Undine, now dead.

Only the submersibles survived, carrying the decimated armada's senior officers and staff to the same sheltered depths. When they once again ascended to augur-depth they found a harbour choked with charred hulks and the waters bobbing with bodies. Worse still was Hive Pherusa. Within hours the hive city had been levelled by the green-skins' barrage of bombs. Now it was just a small mountain of smouldering masonry and wreckage being gradually reclaimed by the waves.

Commander Lux Allegra only knew this because she had been on board the command submersible *Tiamat* when the attack unfolded. She had been summoned by both General Phifer and Admiral Novakovic, although she suspected that Lord Governor Borghesi's gratitude had something to do with the order. It turned out to be an earned but impromptu promotion. Lux Allegra was commander no more. She was Captain Allegra now.

She ached to be with her 'Screeching Eagles'. To tell Goh-landr. But they were gone. By the time she reached the forward airlock, the attack had been under way. Novako-vic had given the order for the submersible contingent to dive. Rocked by the hell at surface-level and the vox-reports coming in from sinking ships and vessels aflame, the *Tia-mat* and her consorts sank to safety.

'Captain Allegra to the conn. Captain Allegra to the conn. Urgent,' the vox-hailer blared. For the longest time, she couldn't make herself move. Her stomach was a knot. Her chest was wracked with a paralysing tension. Her boots felt like they had melted to the metal decking. Her mind was a pict-recording set in a loop. An urchin's existence in the underhive. Gohlandr. Piracy; privateership; recruitment. Gohlandr. Hive Tyche. Gohlandr saving her life. The life inside her that belonged to Lyle Gohlandr. Had belonged to him. Her hand drifted to the flak armour across her belly. She allowed her face to screw up.

'Captain Allegra to the conn. Urgent,' the loudhailer repeated. Allegra's hand fell away from her midriff. She ran the back of the other across her eyes but still found no tears there. She grabbed the support rails set into the alcove sides.

'Get... up,' the captain told herself – and she did. Her mind was numb but her legs were moving. She allowed them to take her to the submersible's conning tower.

There she found a rat's nest of Marineer officers and support staff, Undinians who moved with frenetic urgency and purpose. Guardsmen and women lost in the emergency, who dared not allow themselves a moment to contemplate the unfolding destruction of their home world.

At the heart of the cramped and darkened command centre, she found the Lord Governor. Borghesi sat in his wheeled chair in silence. Gone was the imperious triviality of petty demands. Also missing was the careless entitlement of a spireborn. The Lord Commander now felt the responsibility of one born to the spire, a man born to rule in the Emperor's name. He looked almost as wretched as she did. He didn't avoid her gaze. He didn't say anything. He just pursed his lips and gave her his sad eyes.

Phifer and Novakovic had lost too many men and too many vessels to feel any particular loss that acutely. Like their frantic personnel, they hid behind what was left of their honour and professional responsibility. Allegra found them standing about the faded hololithic representation of the Great Ocean. Hive after hive had fallen. The greenskin invaders were falling like a curtain on Undine, their descent line moving swiftly across the ocean planet. Presented as such, Allegra could see how the hive-world's oceans had been their greatest ally, swallowing innumerable savages and filling the bellies of deep-sea megafauna. If Undine had been a world of rock and dirt, the greenskin monsters would have long since swarmed the planet.

This fact did not make Undine's fate any less desperate. According to the hololith, only the distant western hives of Nemertis, Arethuse and Pontoplex remained untouched by the alien war host. Several isolated patrols were still operating on the turbulent seas of these regions, including the *Meridius* launch carrier group and the Western Marinine base of operations, Port Squall. The base sported a Thunderbolt contingent and two Marauder wings, including the Marinine 1st and 3rd. It was towards Port Squall that Allegra assumed the submersibles were headed. She was wrong.

Novakovic seemed to notice her for the first time. The aged admiral was dressed in his great coat and rubbers. He gave her a grim nod, and she managed an answering salute. Phifer didn't acknowledge her at all. He was known amongst the Marineer officer corps to be a cold bastard but a competent one, and he was the only officer that Allegra knew of that had actually fought off-world. He was staring darkly at the hololith and the story it told. It seemed that the general knew the end and he didn't like it.

'You sent for me, sirs,' Allegra said, wishing that they would send her straight back. She did not quite understand what use she could be to them. Her 'Screeching Eagles' were gone. Her captaincy an empty formality. Perhaps the

Tiamat would reach the *Meridius* battlegroup; perhaps those Marineers left aboard the submersibles could support the Marinine 1st and 3rd in their protection of Hive Arethuse or make a stand at Port Squall. Hive Arethuse wouldn't survive the swarms of hulking invaders clawing their way out of the sea. Port Squall could not hope to stand against the monstrous air superiority of the greenskin bomber wings.

'She sees it,' Novakovic said through the hololithic static.

Phifer nodded, again without looking at the captain. His face was an unreadable mask, taut and fixed.

'She does,' he agreed in his deep, Northern drawl.

'See what?'

'The futility of the situation,' Novakovic said. 'We cannot stand against the magnitude of this threat.'

'The Marineers are a planetary defence force,' Phifer said, 'and we have defended our fair world to the best of our ability. This is, however, an Imperial world. It is part of the Emperor's domain. We must look to the Emperor's faithful subjects on neighbouring worlds to aid us in this desperate hour.'

'How do we know that they haven't been invaded?' Allegra said. 'That they are faring any better than Undine?'

'We don't,' the aged admiral told her.

'The Lord Governor has allowed our regimental astropath to use his consular codes and send requests for aid to Zeta Corona, Farhaven and Triassi Prime. We have also attempted to contact the Mechanicus servants of the Phlogistos Forges and sent word to the Vulpius Crusade, passing through the Weald Worlds. The astropath confirmed that the Black Templars Space Marines received our request for assistance. In all likelihood, the Adeptus Astartes are en route.'

'Sounds hopeful,' Allegra acknowledged, but her voice said anything but.

'The Emperor's Angels were crafted to meet such threats as these,' Novakovic said. 'And the Black Templars are known the galaxy over as great enemies of the alien. Undine will prosper once again in the fires of their hatred. I pity no savage but if I did, I'd pity the greenskins that placed themselves in the Templars' path.'

'But...' Allegra put to them.

'The admiral, the Lord Governor and I have been drafting a contingency,' Phifer said gravely.

'In the event that the Adeptus Astartes do not reach us,' Novakovic clarified.

'We cannot allow the greenskin invader to take Undine,' General Phifer said, his words those of an off-world warlord rather than the sentiments of an ocean homelander. 'We have a responsibility to the Imperium – to the Emperor. Live or die, we must deny the alien this tiny part of the Imperium.'

'I agree, general,' Allegra told him with difficulty, her own losses still gnawing away at her soul. 'But how might such a miracle be procured? Billions live who soon will perish. What weapons we had now sit on the seabed. The enemy is irresistible in savagery and number. They will not be denied.'

'I need a small contingency force,' General Phifer went on, 'led by an officer of character and certitude – one who will do what must be done.'

'General...'

'The Lord Governor gave you as a recommendation,' Phifer told her. 'Your past familiarity with these waters makes you an excellent choice.' The Marineer general focused the hololith in on a tiny island in the middle of the featureless ocean, many leagues from the major hive or pontoon communities. 'You know Desolation Point, of course.'

Allegra nodded. She knew it well. She'd worked as second mate on a gun-rover out of Desolation Point before operating a wrecker under her own captaincy in the surrounding waters. She had both been a pirate and a privateer preying on pirates in and around the half-mythical port. Desolation Point was the buried memory of a former life.

'Apocalytic invasion or not, the Brethren will not fight for Marineers who have spent their life hunting and persecuting them,' Lux Allegra told them.

'You did,' Admiral Novakovic reminded her.

'Those that are not whoring or in their stimm-chests will have heard of the invasion over the vox-waves and taken to the high seas,' Allegra said.

'Like cowards,' the general muttered.

'Like survivors, general,' Allegra corrected him.

'Well, we will be neither,' Novakovic said, 'if the Black Templars don't arrive in time.'

'Which is why we need a contingency plan, captain,' Phifer said. 'There is something at Desolation Point of strategic value, but it is not the good anchorage or the Brethren scum that haunt it.'

'Then what?'

'Did you ever wonder,' Admiral Novakovic put to her, 'why

the Marineers did not simply deploy Marauder wings to blast your island hideout to oblivion?'

'I don't understand, admiral.'

'Desolation Point was the worst kept secret in the Sixteen Seas,' Novakovic told her. 'The Undinian defence forces could have taken it at any time, rather than chasing pirate skiffs all over the ocean and engaging the services of turncoat privateers like yourself.'

'Then why didn't you?' Allegra replied, the edge of a challenge creeping into her voice.

'Because your Brethren,' Phifer said, half-spitting the word, 'chose Desolation Point for its isolated location. Just like the Imperial Army.'

'Excuse me, sir?'

'Your haven of rust and corrugated scrap is built on top of an old Imperial Army depot,' Phifer said. 'The rocky isle was too small for hive foundations but perfect for a small subterranean installation. A storage facility for two-stage orbital munitions and planetary bombs left over from the wars of the Great Heresy. They were hidden and largely forgotten at Desolation Point until the Brethren took the island for their own.'

'We could not take Desolation Point,' Admiral Novakovic said, 'for fear that the Brethren had these weapons in their possession and might use them against the defence force or even the hive populations. You thought you were hidden; in fact, you were untouchable. That is why piracy flourished and the Lord Governor's prosecution of the Brethren was half-hearted at best.'

'I've never heard of such weapons,' Allegra told them.

'It's likely that the Brethren never discovered them,' Nova-kovic said. 'They are secured in a fortified underground depot. We couldn't take the chance, however. We have suffered defections to the Brethren as the pirate lords have to us.' The admiral flashed his eyes.

Lux Allegra didn't care much for ancient history. A bitter fire had returned to belly, however. 'These weapons of mass destruction could be used against the invader,' she said, finally seeing where the Marineer commanders were going with their history lesson.

'After a fashion,' the admiral said cautiously.

'Records show that the cache of stored orbital weapons are largely biologicals,' General Phifer said. 'They fell out of favour with Loyalist forces and a number were secured at Desolation Point.'

'Biologicals.'

'Virus bombs, captain.'

The fire in Allegra's belly felt suddenly doused.

'A contingency force,' she said, repeating the general's earlier words. 'You mean to deny Undine to the invader.'

A gleam of grim determination found its way into Phifer's eyes.

'Should the Adeptus Astartes not arrive in time,' the general said, 'I aim to preserve Undine for the Emperor.'

'Preserve for him a dead rock in space,' Allegra accused.

'A rock purified of the green plague, yes,' Phifer shot back. 'An Imperial rock, captain.'

'What about the Western Hives?' Allegra said, turning to Lord Governor Borghesi. 'The billions at Pontoplex, Nemertis, Arethuse?'

The old man shook his head sadly.

'No one will survive the biological weapons, once they are unleashed,' Phifer said. 'But no one will survive the invader, and it has already been unleashed.'

Lux Allegra was silent. She couldn't fully imagine the enormity of the act Phifer, Novakovic and Borghesi were proposing. She felt the cold comfort of a fate accepted creep into her bones. Her hand unconsciously drifted down to the flak armour over her stomach. All of sudden, Lyle Gohlandr didn't feel so far away.

'We talk of contingency, captain,' Admiral Novakovic said. 'Hopefully, the Black Templars will arrive in time and the Emperor's Angels will deliver precious Undine.'

'Captain?' Phifer said.

'I'll do it,' Allegra replied icily.

The old men – general, admiral and governor all – nodded silently.

A kind of terrible calm descended.

'My men are dead,' Allegra said at length. It felt strange to actually say the words.

'You can take my security detail,' General Phifer said. 'Commander Tyrhone?'

An officer stepped forwards from the shadows of the tiny command centre. He was dressed in the charcoal uniform of the Marineer Elites and had the dark skin of a Southern hiver. His face was all jutting bones and unsmiling gristle. A man made hard by his duties and the needs of the general under whom he served.

'Tyrhone and his squad will be at your disposal,' General Phifer said. 'The commander will be of use to you in priming

the virus bombs for a launchless detonation.' Allegra nodded at the commander, who said nothing. Phifer gave her
a data-slate. 'This contains the location and security codes
for the depot hatch-entrance. We cannot guarantee easy
movement across the island. Desolation Point is a small
colony but will still no doubt attract landing enemy in voracious number.'

'Just get me as close to the shore as you can,' Allegra said.
'The north-east anchorage is the deepest and traditionally
admits submersibles.'

'Hold the depot,' General Phifer ordered. 'Prime the biologicals and await my command. Do you think you can do
that?'

Allegra turned with the data-slate in hand and made for
the conning tower airlock.

'Like I said,' she said, half to herself, 'I'll do it.'

FIFTEEN

Eidolica – Alcazar Astra

It was a wall of green flesh. A perimeter of brawn, bone and armour. An enclosure of savagery and xenos hatred. The genetic forefathers of the Fists Exemplar had stood on the walls of the Imperial Palace during the Battle of Terra. All of Dorn's sons knew what it took to defend a wall and what it took to bring one crashing down.

Second Captain Maximus Thane knew. But despite bringing wall after greenskin wall toppling to the hull of the star fort in clouds of gore and splinter-showers of skull, Thane always found that another beast-wall had been erected behind the bloody ruins in its place.

It had been carnage for the past hour. The *Alcazar Astra* trembled with the storming footfalls of the alien invader. Battle-brothers stood their ground on the thick void plating of the fortress-monastery's hull, with wild blades and bullets sparking off the scorched surface of their armour. The greenskins were everywhere, smothering the fallen star fort with their foul, alien presence. The Space Marines fought for

their commanders. They fought for their companies. They fought for their Chapter and their fortress-monastery. They fought for their world. Like the metal gargoyles adorning what had been the star fort's void ramparts, the Adeptus Astartes refused to move. They would not allow their defensive lines to be broken. But the green tide was irresistible as it washed monstrosities up from the sands and across the monastery decking, flooding each mighty transept with innumerable targets.

As Maximus Thane ducked and weaved, kicked and blasted, he felt like the fortress-monastery was sinking. Not below the sands, but below the great number of the enemy. There was green everywhere. Savage after savage came at him and the Space Marines of his honoured company. Inside his helmet it was no better. There too he was drowning in reports and requests, his suit filtering vox-transmissions from his own desperate men over a cacophony of communications coming from Fists Exemplar brothers holding the rest of the fort's perimeter. It seemed that the alien brutes were pressing the defenders from all sides simultaneously, with muscle to spare and a constant stream of reinforcements.

Hugging his Umbra-pattern boltgun close into his shoulder, Thane felt the kick of the honourable weapon. Like a beast of burden thrashing and bucking its way to freedom, it wanted to be let loose on the enemy, but ammunition was precious. No battle-brother could know for how long he or his bolter would be needed. It was better to conserve the blessed shells than bury them in alien cadavers already finding their way to the ground.

With his elbows out and boltgun tucked in close to his plate, the captain smashed his way through the walls of alien meat. Blood and snaggle-teeth flew from where Thane buried the elbow couter-joints of his suit into snarling green faces. Guts spilled from towering behemoths whose swollen bellies came in line with the squat barrel of his gun. A beast came at him from the left, a hydraulically augmented nightmare from the right. An axe of some brute description sang off his pauldron. A hulking greenskin, struggling to bring its steaming rotor cannon under control, managed to sink lead into the flesh of the mongrel-monsters attempting to tackle Thane to the ground. The captain's plate registered the impact of several glancing rotor shells before swiftly reporting an update of full suit integrity in his visor display. Thane brought his boltgun up.

Unlike the rotor-gunning greenskin, he did not miss his target. A judicious staccato of shells opened the beast's skull up like an oasis fruit. With vicious momentum, the captain smashed the orks coming at him from the side back into their ranks. The first was trampled under the boots of its gore-hungry comrades. The second soaked up several suit-augmented impacts before Thane's elbow broke through its helmet, hydraulics and skull.

Between the split-second ducking, dodging and evasive footwork – and when he wasn't forced to end some mindless, oncoming brute – the captain attempted to cast his gaze about the swarming transept. Several battle-brothers had gone down. He'd seen Brothers Vaux and Martegan both murdered by the same power-clawed monstrosity.

'Sergeant Hoque,' Thane voxed. 'Get those battle-brothers back on the ramparts.'

'Yes, sir,' Hoque voxed back, the ferocious chatter of his bolter in the background.

'A step back towards the hangar bays is a step in retreat,' the captain called. 'Let that be on the conscience of any battle-brother indulging such a notion.'

'Yes, sir,' Hoque returned, his voice once again lost in desperate bolt fire.

Thane took the heads off three advancing creatures with his boltgun while a fourth sprayed the Fists Exemplar with lead from its own crude automatic weapon.

'Brother Aquino,' Thane said. 'Stop playing with that thing and end it swiftly. The enemy are pushing through.'

'Yes, captain.'

Sparks rained off the captain's plate as the lead-sprayer closed. Smashing the weapon aside with his own, Thane found that the primitive death-dealer came apart with relative ease. Trusting in the craftsmanship of his own weapon, the captain stabbed its muzzle into the creature's jaw, taking out a lump of flesh. Momentarily dazed, the monster reached for another weapon from its sagging belt. Its claw never got there, however. Thane had shot it through the eye and was pushing past it before the greenskin's carcass hit the hull.

'Squad Autolycon, Squad Lucifus, close that gap!' the captain bawled across the vox-channel. 'You could get a Land Raider through there.'

'We could use a Land Raider up here,' a battle-brother voxed between sword-swinging exertions.

'Secure your mouth, brother,' Sergeant Hoque bit back.
'Keep your mind on your work and follow your captain's
commands.'

As Thane blasted through two more greenskin savages, he
was forced to admit that the battle-brother was right. Chapter Land Raiders would have done a nice job of breaking
up the greenskin swarms on the dunes. Their heavy bolters would have crashed through the monstrous lines. Their
lascannons would have cut through the dense formations.
Their tracks would have mulched the green invader into the
black Eidolican sands. They would have created an advancing line of rally points, allowing the Fists Exemplar to push
the enemy vanguard back.

That was all fantasy now. Chapter Master Alameda had
gone out to meet the first wave of greenskins on the Fortunata Flats as they thundered from the black desert-world
skies. Anticipating that the xenos would fight from the fortifications of their rocks and landing hulks, the Chapter
Master had brought tracked fortifications of his own, in
the form of the Chapter's Land Raiders. A second wave of
descents had landed almost on top of the first, however.
While having the virtue of smashing many of the rocks
and accompanying barbarian mobs into the desert pen-
insula, the second-wave descent also pulverised the Land
Raider formation. Tanks were buried beneath rocks. Tanks
were smashed to ruins. Tanks were bounced and toppled
by the impact quakes of landing hulks. The formation
scattered, while the crews of other partially immobilised
vehicles were forced to fall back to exposed holdpoints in
the dunes. Chapter Master Alameda wasn't among them.

His command vehicle had been one of the first smashed into the sands.

Thane couldn't imagine how many waves there had been since that dark hour. Fifty? Perhaps a hundred. Barely a handful of Land Raiders had made it back, and those were sent on immediately by First Captain Garthas to support Captain Dentor fighting on the Tharkis Flats and in the Great Basin.

Two great arms suddenly wrapped around the captain. Something had seized Thane from behind. The arms were thick and scarred, and Thane felt like he was in the embrace of one of the *Alcazar Astra*'s redundant void-docking anchors as he was lifted off the deck of the star fort. A huge ork had reared to its full height and had taken him towards the heavens with it. The deluge of green fury swept in beneath Thane, hacking at the captain's thrashing boots with chain-choppers and great axes.

Thane's plate was telling him something alarming about the hulk's colossal embrace and its effect on the suit's integrity. He could hear the creak of ceramite about him and the strain of servos. Above him the monster's elephantine skull belted out a roar of triumph, something to enrage the sea of green about it to savage jubilation, before it acted upon its intention to crush the Adeptus Astartes like a cheap alloy can.

Thane felt the monster tense further. His auto-senses registered a rapid descent, and before he knew it he was back on the hull of the *Alcazar Astra*. The creature had released him, and the captain was free. Descending further to one ceramite knee, Thane turned in the gore, his boltgun ready to blast a crater in the gargantuan thing.

He found that the giant greenskin's legs had been taken out from under it. The creature had nothing below its knees and had fallen down onto the bloody stumps. As it toppled forwards onto all fours, Thane saw Apothecary Reoch standing behind the beast. Reoch had been responsible for the sweeping amputation. His armour was dripping with blood, but his chainsword gleamed like a surgical tool. The Apothecary stomped forwards, hacking down on the maimed creature, executing precision strikes like a living autopsy on the beast-ork. It roared its rage and frustration briefly before the Apothecary worked his way up to the fang-mangled skull of the thing and took it off at the neck.

'Back!' Maximus Thane bawled as he slid back around on his knee. Behind him he found the wall of green once more. 'Back... Back...Back!' he called, his commands accompanied by single bolt-rounds of persuasion. One by one, the rushing oncomers dropped before the weapon's fury.

A Thunderhawk swooped above them, hammering into the masses with its heavy bolters. The gunship cut a path of mulched ork-flesh through the enemy lines, taking with it the next few beasts in line for Thane's vengeance. The Thunderhawks were doing what they always did: performing admirably. They were inflicting horrific casualties on the invasion host, but the impact of their bloody work was neither seen nor felt by the battle-brothers on the ground. The orks weren't impressed by the gunships or their death-delivering ordnance. The roar of the Mars-pattern engines and the punishment of their heavy guns and cannons drove the monsters into fits of exultant rage. As a homogenous war host, the ork invaders resembled some kind of mythical beast. Where one creature fell, two others would charge from the throngs in its place.

Standing once more, Thane felt his power pack brush against the Apothecary's. The pair fought back to back – Reoch opening up monsters with precision and Thane finding his way to single-shot kills with his brutal bolter fire.

'Mortalities?' Thane called across the helmet vox.

'Fourteen that have been relayed to my suit,' Reoch replied, gunning his chainsword in neat arcs.

'I thought worse than that.'

'You're relieved by the number,' the Apothecary said. 'You shouldn't be. Do the arithmetic: we won't see the dawn.'

Ducking beneath the irresistible orbit of a crude hammer, Thane slammed his boltgun into the wielder's gut. Pushing against the creature with his suit-augmented might, the Fists Exemplar Space Marine made a little space between himself and the alien. Not much. There were a thousand other monsters behind it howling for their transhuman blood. It had, however, created enough of a gap to bring up the boltgun and blast several ragged holes into the greenskin's chest. The ork fell back into the roaring green masses.

'Well, the good news,' Reoch told him, 'is that our losses are fewer than on the other transepts. Hieronimax is down a quarter strength. Xontague nearly a half.'

'Holy Throne...' Thane hissed. Then, 'Reloading!'

Reoch stretched himself to keep the beasts from his captain. Driving the chainsword through one monster, he reverse-gunned the weapon and sawed it through the limbs of two other unfortunates. Then once again the hammer came at them. The monster swinging it was back, despite having a bolt-blasted ribcage. The heavy metal weapon came over the ork's howling head and straight down at the Space Marines. Moving aside and away from one another, Thane and Reoch allowed the head of the weapon to smash into the void hull, where the captain fancied it might have even dented the armour plating. The Apothecary put a boot on the hammer and proceeded to saw through the weapon's reinforced shaft.

'The head,' Reoch suggested.

Thane nodded. The thing's ugly features were staring at the deck, its eyes following the hammer and the mess the monster had hoped it would make of the Adeptus Astartes. Priming the boltgun, Thane stared down his sights before blasting the ork up under its chin and through the back of its skull. This time the beast fell away for good.

With their attention on the hammer-wielding savage, the captain and Apothecary had allowed the crushing swarms of orks to crowd them once more. Thane's disciplined bolt blasts were now at almost point-blank range. Reoch had little space to conduct his surgical dismemberments and was forced to snatch one of his bolt pistols from a thigh holster and show off his own close-quarter marksmanship.

A heavy axe, cut brutally from a single piece of vessel hull-decking, found Thane momentarily wanting. It smashed the captain to one side, breaching the plate of his pauldron and sending one of his bolt-rounds wide. It took a second or so for Thane to recover but by then both axe-swinger and bolt-survivor were upon him, the creatures hacking away at the captain's honourable plate. The monsters roared. Thane roared back, throwing himself at the gigantic specimens. Grabbing one of the beasts by a shoulder-spike, he buried the muzzle of his boltgun in the ork's pot-bellied abdomen. Blasting several rounds into the greenskin's gut, he allowed the alien to fall, clutching at its ruined midriff with its claws. Almost immediately, Thane brought the boltgun up and blasted through the throat of the second. It dropped to reveal the partially obscured shape of a larger monster behind.

'This isn't working,' Thane said across the vox.

'You don't have to tell me,' Reoch replied, sweeping his chainsword about him in tight arcs of flesh-carving efficiency.

'Oratorium,' Thane switched channel, 'this is Second Captain Thane, Transept West.'

'Yes, captain,' a voice returned. It didn't belong to the First Captain.

'Where's Garthas?'

Thane brought down the hulking ork before him. It took three bolts, which was more ammunition than he had budgeted for the task. He helm-butted a smaller warrior-wretch and smashed in the skull of a third with the clutched gauntlet-grip of his boltgun. Alien brains speckled his plate.

'We suffered a breach, captain,' the oratorium replied. 'Fortress-Monastery North. Captain Hieronimax is down. The First Captain went to repel the breach force with the Chapter Master's honour guard and support the Ninth.'

'Sounds like Garthas,' Reoch added across a private channel, with simultaneous hints of derision and respect.

'To whom do I speak?' Thane said.

Another greenskin died. Then another. And another.

'Brother Zerberyn, captain.'

Thane recognised the name. A member of Alameda's hon-our guard. The warriors fighting at the First Captain's side, Fortress Monastery North.

'Are you injured, honoured brother?'

'At Fortunata, captain,' Zerberyn replied.

'Brother,' Thane said, 'we are hard pressed to gain any ground here. The void ramparts are swarming with green-skins. Can Captain Tyrian spare brothers for a front-line repulsion? We have to push these savages back into range of our weapons. Then we might be able to hold them there.'

'Negative, captain,' Zerberyn said. 'The First Captain's orders were very specific. All companies to hold their own fronts. He did not want resulting strategic weaknesses to lead to breach actions.'

'We already have breach actions,' Thane snapped back. As the captain spoke, the killing continued.

'And we cannot afford another,' Zerberyn said. 'I'm sorry, sir. These are the First Captain's orders. I would no more countermand them than your own.'

'What about the guns?' Apothecary Reoch barked, slash-ing back the beasts with one hand, while plugging charging green swine in the face with the bolt pistol clutched furi-ously in his other.

'The rampart guns are silent,' Thane relayed. Indeed, the mega-bolters and gatling-blaster emplacements had smoked to a stop some time before. Their absence had been keenly felt by the Fists Exemplar on the West Transept.

'Master Aloysian ordered the weapons to cease firing, sir,' Zerberyn reported. 'The Master of the Forge observed protocols recognising that fighting on the ramparts had become a close-quarters engagement. The guns were silenced in order that no battle-brothers be harmed by the star fort's weaponry.'

'We'll risk it,' Reoch growled.

'Return the guns to operation,' Thane commanded.

'The Master's orders, sir,' Zerberyn replied. 'His protocols won't allow it.'

'Are we to die out here by regulation and protocol?' Thane called back. 'Patch me through to Master Aloysian.'

'As you wish, captain.'

'I fear he enjoyed that,' Reoch said of the officious Zerberyn.

Thane had other problems. His boltgun was empty. Like many of his brother Fists, he would need resupplying, and soon. There was no time for such expediency, however. Swamped by greenskins clambering over the corpses of their barbarian kin, Thane had used the final few rounds of the sickle magazine to take the momentum out of a rabid charge mounted by a suicidal throng of alien monstrosities. He didn't even have the precious moments it would take to recover his final clip, mag-locked to the rear of his belt. The mob of orks surrounding the captain were met with thrashing elbows and the stamp of armoured boots. Ducking instruments of bludgeoning improvisation and allowing the broad blades of crude machetes to glance off his pauldrons, Thane tried to give back as much savagery and violence as was being collectively bestowed on him.

'Master Aloysian?'

'Yes, second captain,' the Master of the Forge returned.

Thane tried to imagine the Techmarine in the generatorium, at the head of an army of drone-brained servitors, a perpetual scowl buried in the white of his beard.

'Master, I need the rampart guns to visit Dorn's ire on the enemy once more,' Thane put to him. The captain brought down a beast with a power-armoured sweep of one leg before stamping down on the throat of the prone creature with the sole of his boot. It took several determined stomps to crush down through the gristle and iron-hard muscle of the greenskin's neck.

'Impossible, captain,' Aloysian told him.

'That's not acceptable, Master Aloysian. I don't care for the letter of your protocols: we need those guns.'

'Their protocols are runic,' Aloysian called back. 'They will not compromise their own observances. And those observances exist to preserve life.'

'Life is not being preserved out here, Master Aloysian, I can assure you of that.'

'Captain,' the Techmarine returned, 'I can't do anything for you. Each holy weapon would need catechising by hand. Besides, I've sent the gun crews to Fortress Monastery North to establish barricades and corridor emplacements.'

'What *can* the generatorium do for us?' Thane asked bitterly. 'The enemy is upon us as a relentless force. Our weapons run dry and battle-brothers are dying in their droves.'

'Little, captain,' Aloysian said with regret. 'Once the *Alcazar Astra* was an instrument of preservation. A great weapon among the stars. Now, the fort is an instrument to be preserved. An objective to be garrisoned and guarded. As a fortress-home, it serves with honour. But great weapon of the void it is no more.'

Thane dwelled on the forge master's words. He thought on the *Alcazar Astra* restored to her former glory, her great engines turning her graceful bulk to present her batteries of void cannon to the armada junkships of the alien invader. He momentarily lived the pure obliteration the star fort could visit on hulks and landers packed to their rattletrap airlocks with hulking greenskins. Invaders it would take hours to meat-grind through in the ramparts could be void-scorched in moments in orbit.

Thane's fantasy had cost him. A towering brute of a greenskin – repugnant, even by the standards of its breed – battered two ork bully-boys aside to get to the captain. It swung a length of sharpened girder in its hulking claws like a broadsword. The irresistible path of the heavy blade swooped underneath Thane's elbow and smashed the captain to one side, cleaving the ceramite of his torso into crumpled plating. Auto-senses within his helm went wild. The girder-blade came down at Thane from above. It didn't have the same orbital force as the first blow but all the captain had to offer in defence was his forearm plate, his empty boltgun still held tightly in his gauntlets. Slicing into the plate of the defending arm, the monstrous ork cut down at the captain as he knelt on one armoured knee.

The Apothecary's gleaming chainblade was suddenly between them. The glint of its monomolecular teeth seemed to grab the beast's attention. It swung the girder-blade at Reoch, the Apothecary defending as elegantly as a battle-brother might against such force and ferocity. Slicing and lopping at each other – the savage not seeming to notice the bite of the chainsword's tip – the pair clashed blades. Holding the chainsword out in front of him, Reoch gunned it to a screeching blur.

Sparks showered the pair. The girder must have been made of some reinforced alloy, something scavenged by the creature from a crashed vessel. The chainblade was struggling against the material, and the ork used the difficulty to put its full weight behind the crude edge. The brute pushed with all its savage might, sending Reoch tumbling back into a knot of smaller creatures.

By the time it returned its barbaric attentions to Thane, the captain was back on his feet. The girder-blade came up. The tusked maw snarled. A battle-brother was suddenly there to defend his captain, his boltgun blazing, but the monster absently cleaved the Space Marine in two.

'Captain!' a second Fist Exemplar called. His weapon was spent also, and he cut deep into the creature's green flesh with a gladius blade. The colossal ork's arm shot out and grabbed the Space Marine by the helmet. His entire head was lost in the thing's claw. The battle-brother dropped both empty boltgun and sword. His limbs thrashed furiously as the monstrous ork crushed his helm and tossed his armoured body out into the killing fields of its kin.

The beast was back on Thane in an instant. Its mongrel weapon rose. Thane brought up his boltgun. The length of the weapon was all he had to put between him and the sword's mangling impact, but the captain suddenly jabbed the boltgun forwards, smashing into the greenskin's tusk-crowded jaws with the empty sickle-clip. Thumbing the ejection stud, Thane retracted the boltgun, leaving the magazine embedded in the beast's fractured face.

The broadsword came down. Thane stepped aside, and drew back his right gauntlet. Leaning into the servo-supported punch, Maximus Thane slammed his fist into the clip, hammering it into the monster's skull. The girder-blade rang to the deck first, followed swiftly by the small green mountain of the ork's corpse.

Snatching his remaining magazine from his belt and slamming it home, Thane blasted several greenskin savages clear of the struggling Apothecary. The remaining beasts fell to a three-hundred-and-sixty degree spin that Reoch accomplished with his chainsword, aided by the slick of gore on the void hull surface.

'Captain?' the Master of the Forge called. 'Captain, are you still there?'

'Yes, Master Aloysian,' Thane replied, 'but not for much longer. We have to force the enemy back to range. The alien are too many and we are too few to take them one at a time. As Apothecary Reoch says, the arithmetic doesn't add up.'

'What can I do, captain?'

'You can activate the *Alcazar Astra*'s remaining plasma drive.'

'Captain?'

'Are you hearing me, Aloysian?' Thane called across the vox-channel. 'I want you to fire the Transept East engine column.'

'But captain,' the Master of the Forge protested, 'the star fort is buried in a crater of its own making. It cannot ascend on one engine alone.'

'Can it be done?' Thane demanded.

'The fortress-monastery's superstructure will suffer damage.'

'Would you rather the invader demolish it instead?'

'The fort will incline, not ascend, captain,' the Techmarine insisted.

'I certainly hope so,' Maximus Thane said.

Sliding about in the gore, his chainsword singing its way through tough, alien flesh, Reoch allowed himself a grunt of realisation and agreement.

'I should vox the First Captain,' Master Aloysian said.

'Captain Garthas is busy,' Thane told him. 'I am ranking brother on the ramparts and this strategy concerns their very orientation.'

'Yes, captain.'

'As soon as possible, Master Aloysian,' Thane added. 'Brother Fists will pay for any delay.'

'Yes, captain.'

Crashing bolts through the greenskins throwing themselves at him, Thane smashed and skidded his way back to Apothecary Reoch.

'Brother Zerberyn,' the second captain voxed to the injured honorarius.

'Captain?'

'I want you to vox all companies and captains with the following order,' Thane said. Before the battle-brother could protest, Thane added, 'And if you don't, Brother Zerberyn, in less than a minute you'll very much wish you had.'

'What's the order?' Zerberyn crackled back after a moment's hesitation.

'All Fists Exemplar battle-brothers to mag-lock their boots to the void hull.'

'Why?' the honour guard Space Marine voxed back.

Once again, the Apothecary and the captain's packs brushed. Back to back, the Fists Exemplar Space Marines carved and blasted an open space in the green edifice of muscle and savagery surrounding them. An island of life – raw and desperate – in a sea of alien barbarity and death. Four gore-spattering *clunks*, one after another, echoed about the carnage as Thane and Reoch mag-locked their armoured boots to the blood-slick deck.

'Why?' Thane voxed back to Zerberyn. 'Because we are going for a ride.'

SIXTEEN

Undine – Desolation Point

The north-eastern anchorage was treacherous but, as Allegra had indicated, deep enough to admit the submerged draught of the *Tiamat*. With little else but the conning tower breaking the surface, Captain Lux Allegra accompanied Commander Tyrhone's Marineer Elites out onto the small observation deck. The Elites carried garrison-duty dirks and stubby lascarbines, slung in waterproof casings.

The grating was awash with the chemical brume that passed for seawater on Undine. The commander and several other Elites had hauled personal sweeps up onto the deck. The sweeps were one-man watercraft: lightweight planers that consisted of a pontoon chassis, steering bars and a high-power churnfan. Setting off towards the colony outcrop that was Desolation Point on the sweeps, the watercraft's riders dragged behind them wire ladders to which Allegra and the other Elites clung.

The sky was streaming with rocks and crash-capsules, falling towards the ocean surface. Fountains of spray erupted from impact sites. The greenskin descent wave had reached Desolation Point before them.

As Allegra had predicted, the anchorage was largely deserted. Vox-casts would have warned the many denizens of the marauder colony of the horror to come. Those with grapnel-rigs, solarjammers and Q-craft took to the seas, taking as many with them as could afford to leave the island. Even now, vessels were streaming out of port: smoke-belching outriggers, armed freighters and plasteel-clad sloops.

Although they remained low in the water and were not advertising their presence, Allegra and the Elites didn't need to avoid such pirate vessels on their shoreline approach. Each was being horrifically boarded. As green alien hulks hauled themselves up the vessels they tore pieces off them and swamped the decks with brutality and carnage. The creatures soaked up canister-shot from pintle-mounted deck weapons and made short work of pistol-blazing raiders – who eventually had little choice but to climb for their towers and rigging.

The colony itself – a fragile accretion of scrap, adapted giga-containers and chain walkways – had been well on its way to becoming a proto-hive. The restrictions of the island bedrock meant that designs became more vertiginous and the rising architecture increasingly perilous. Fires were feeling their way through the pirate haven, with smoke snaking from underbuildings and corrugated citadels. As Commander Tyrhone guided his sweep through the choppy waters of the evacuating anchorage, Allegra held on tight, her eyes kept busy with the demise of Desolation Point.

The captain had not got off to the best start with the Elites. There had been several reasons for this. Firstly, like Tyrhone, they largely hailed from the Southern hives and so were naturally suspicious of a salt-pale Northerner like Allegra. Her tattoos and piercings marked her out as being a turn-coat: a pirate turned privateer. The kind of scum that real Marineers like Tyrhone and his men traditionally hunted. Her Marineer rank, similarly, had little meaning for them either. Her 'Screeching Eagles' had been grunt coastals and boardsmen, not the highly-trained tacticals that General Phifer retained for his security detail.

The final insult was Allegra's insistence that they eat before they set off on their mission. Tyrhone told her that he didn't expect the operation to last long enough to warrant rations, while his men gave her jaundiced glares. Besides, if needed, Elites could live off the ocean for as long as the mission dictated. Allegra had been forced to make her insistence an order and gave each Marineer a rations can of toonweed. Several refused to eat the pungent mush, until Tyrhone too made it an order to do so. Toonweed, while cheap and nutritious, was considered a pauper's dish by the mezzo-hivers, since it got its name from the crop-forests that grew on the bottom of roving pontoon shanties. Coming largely from sub-spire military families, the Elites regarded the stinking slaw with disgust.

As the sweeps churned away, dragging the Marineer Elites, *Tiamat* dropped back below the waves. Commander Tyrhone wasted no time in making a direct approach, but Allegra directed him towards the bare rock of a jagged spit on the anchorage side. As the sweeps drew closer, it became apparent to the Elites that the rocky shoreline of the island was awash with greenskin beasts, clawing their way out of the sea and shaking water from their brute weaponry. Pockets of resistence were evident across the haven, with the ocean-world pirates employing the island's defences against the greenskin invaders, rather than the enemy for which they were intended – planetary defence and security forces like the approaching Marineer Elites. The spit seemed relatively sparse of alien invaders, and it soon became clear to the Elites why.

The water about the spit seemed agitated, and it had nothing to do with the currents or rock formations about the coastline. Like thick, rubbery propeller screws, a school-pack of helicondra surged for the shale beach. Long, muscular serpentforms, the native creatures cut through the water in a helical, spiral motion. They were prey for many of the ocean world's marine megafauna, but also predators in their own right. They whirled their way through the shallows until, forming rigid, rubbery shafts, they surged up the shale beach to snatch flippered marine mammals from a dog-colony that existed on the spit. The blubber-dog meat was greasily repugnant and not favoured by the inhabitants of Desolation Point. The helicondra pack, however, would reach up the beach like a single, tentacular beast, slithering around surprised blubber-dogs and their pups before dragging them back to the shallows for unfussy ingestion.

As Tyrhone cautiously led the sweeps towards the shale, the Elites could see that the water was bobbing with distended serpents, dazed, full and floating after devouring the bounty of greenskins unfortunate enough to choose the spit as their approach to the haven. Other monsters could be seen on the beach, set upon by three or four of the rubbery constrictors, each attempting the swallow the aliens there on the shale. With arms and legs disappearing down the rippling lengths of the serpents and the helicondra crushing bones and ribcages underneath their knots and coils, the orks were thinning out on the spit.

A serpentine head suddenly shot from the water and hit Tyrhone's sweep and drag-ladder broadside. The helicondra elegantly snatched the Elite behind Allegra on the wire ladder and took the screaming Marineer below the waves on the other side. The full length of the animal proceeded to coil about the vehicle without touching the sweep, drag or other Elites. The soldiers behind Allegra began to reach for their dirks and Tyrhone slowed the sweep.

The captain remembered the man behind her as a smirking soldier who had refused to eat his rations. 'He didn't eat the toonweed,' Allegra called, casting a look behind her and then forwards at the commander who had peered around angrily. Whether he was furious with Allegra or the unfortunate Marineer, it was hard to tell. 'The serpents have a sensitive sense of smell. They can't stand the weed.' She turned back to Tyrhone. 'It's what keeps the islanders safe from attacks,' she gestured at the spit, 'and makes the invader vulnerable. Beach us there.'

Allegra pointed to a bare patch of shale nearby. Unconvinced, but with little choice but to trust the former pirate's local knowledge, Commander Tyrhone led the sweeps up onto the shale beach. Once on the shore, the Elites fell to frantically extracting their lascarbines from their

waterproof cases and assembling silencers and frequency flash-suppressors. With one eye on the chemical surf for surging serpents and the other on their assemblage, the Elites seemed nervous. Crouching in the bleached shale, Allegra watched greenskins dragged back into the water by muscular lengths of helicondra and heard the wet barks of blubber-dogs further up the spit sounding the alarm for their colony. Commander Tyrhone carried two carbines, and was assembling them twice as fast as the rest of his men. Taking one for himself and throwing Allegra the other, Tyrhone pointed to the breech of his weapon as demonstration.

'Suppressor,' he indicated, then moved a dark digit to a megathule modulator. 'Set to a spectral frequency outside of visible range.'

Allegra nodded. Her production-line Marineer lasrifle had sported no such feature. It was going to be difficult shooting without a searing beam to guide her.

'Just look for the smouldering bodies,' Tyrhone said.

Allegra nodded again before making her way up the shale bank. The commander followed, leading his Elites. They all moved swiftly but cautiously, their barrels following their eyes as they scanned the beach for hostiles.

It soon became clear to even the most prejudiced of the mezzohivers that the sea-scum captain had saved them both ammunition and encounters with the enemy. Every greenskin hulk they passed being dragged back through the shale, or being slowly coil-crushed and devoured, would have had to have been killed by the Marineers. Allegra led the way along the spit and through the barking packs of terrified blubber-dogs. The storage dumps and black markets lining the haven shore were ablaze. Precious goods and raided cargoes were furious with flame and the thickset alien thugs were bulldozing their way through the labyrinth of stalls and harbour-bound stocks.

It was unclear whether the greenskins had set the haven alight or whether the remaining pirates had. Many raiders had worked out of Desolation Point their whole lives and would have been loath to give it up to an alien invader. Some determined resistance was being mounted in the accretion squares, mezzanine chem-distilleries and obscura dens. Mostly what Allegra saw of her marauder-kin, however, as the Elites moved silently through the maze of corrugation and scrap, were whores and young rovers being hacked to pieces by greenskin savages.

As the contingency force made their way through the Brethren haven, the captain recognised locations from a childhood spent climbing, swinging and jumping from one salvage-building to another. A rattling refrigeration vault from where she used to steal ichthid eggs. The needle-den where she received a crude tattoo commemorating her second berth on a pirate vessel. A scud-wrestling den where she saw her first life taken.

All Tyrhone had said about the Imperial Army storage depot was that it had a central location. So that was where Allegra led them. Through habstacks, across bridge alleyways and through street-strata, the Marineer Elites negotiated a colony under siege. Where they could, Tyrhone and his men avoided firefights and ramshackle fortifications. Where the gutter-mouths of raiders could be heard bawling curses at invading hulks and the brute chug of greenskin weaponry chewed through corrugated walls and foundation-pillars, the Elites pulled back and had Allegra lead them a different way. They were not outfitted to wage war amongst the haven habitations. They were equipped for a singular mission and purpose.

On the occasions when ork barbarians could not be avoided or simply tusk-charged their way through walls and scrap-metal frontage, the Elites fell to their work with determination and economy. Although their lascarbines betrayed nothing but the drumming stub of automatic fire, beams transparent and invisible, their collective marksmanship was revealed in the thrashing impacts burning into greenskin unfortunates and the smouldering fall of alien cadavers. With such weapons, it took a cumulative and communal effort to kill just one of the beasts, but the Elites' fire discipline and the economy and efficiency of their purpose was beyond question.

Jangling lightly across chain walkways and descending into a much older morass of crushed habitations and reinforced underpassages, Allegra led Commander Tyrhone and his Elites to the centre of Desolation Point: a high-rise aggregation of obscura dens, infusion houses and bordellos. At the captain's confirmation of such, Commander Tyrhone produced a tracking-auspex to scan for munitions signatures. After a moment, the auspex told him that there were indeed munitions in reasonable quantities matching the old Imperial Army signatures of the depot cache, but they were deep below.

'This goes down?' Tyrhone queried.

'A number of sub-levels,' Allegra recalled.

At the haven centre, the greenskins were absent in any number. The same could not be said for raiders and marauders. Desolation Point was the closest thing any of them had to a home. They were not going to give it up to the newly arrived alien invader. Nor the enemy of old, the Undine security forces.

'Get them snappers on the deck,' a voice called from above. The accent was thick and guttural.

The Elites tensed, their eyes down the lengths of their lascarbines, barrels aimed up and down the length and height of the street. A number of marauder gunhands were making their way down a mesh stairwell, holding high-powered autorifles and working bolt actions with grim menace. There were others on balcony walkways and patchwork roofs. Most had heavy-duty sights, but one or two even sported cracked scopes on their scuffed plas-stock rifles.

'I said get 'em down in the rust,' the voice came again. Their skipper stepped out onto the street. Like his men he was all tattoos and dreadlocks, but indulged the extravagance of a grand hat and coat. His coarse hand rested on the grip of a fat stub revolver that nestled in his thick belt.

'We don't have time for this,' Commander Tyrhone told Allegra.

'What do you want me to do?' the captain said absently. It seemed, improbably, that her attention was elsewhere.

'They are the Brethren. They are your people,' the commander pressed, his lascarbine moving between the skipper and the two shotgun-wielding bodyguards that had walked out casually to flank him.

'Do you think we have a secret handshake or something?'

'That's exactly what I thought.'

'Sorry to disappoint you, commander,' Allegra said, her eyes travelling up beyond the death-trap balconies and mesh catwalks. 'These men are Brethren, that's true. But they're also stone cold killers. They'll try to end us, whatever we do. Words will just antagonise them further.'

'I'm gonna count to three,' the skipper spat. His men trained their weapons on the Marineers. The Elites trained their lascarbines back. Allegra returned her eyes to the narrow strip of sky visible up through the chainwalks, meshing and steep-sided accretions. She had been watching something above them. 'One.'

'When the signal is given,' the captain said to the Marineers, 'make your way swiftly down through the sub-levels.'

'What's the signal?' the commander wanted to know.

'Two.'

'You'll know it when you hear it,' Allegra replied.

'Three,' the Brethren skipper snarled. Allegra saw him go for his stub gun. He would have got to it too, if it hadn't been for the impact.

With so many crash-capsules and rocks smacking into the surrounding ocean, it was only a matter of time before one actually struck the island colony itself. Allegra had been tracking the oily smear of the rock's descent, watching it grow bigger and more imminent. By the captain's estimation it hit somewhere on the eastern side of Desolation Point, but it had been a hard landing: rock on rock. The impact was ear-splitting. The immediate shockwave was enough to violently tremble through balconies, walkways and accretion structures.

As the skipper and his pirate gunhands became

preoccupied with the instability of their surroundings, Commander Tyrhone and his Elite Marineers did as they were ordered. They dropped down through cutways and ladderwells onto the sub-level below with their captain. As Allegra led them down through the dank meshways and underpasses, the soldiers could hear the howl of the impact gales above, whipping through the insanity of the architecture. This was followed swiftly by the cacophonous boom and excruciating moan of metalwork twisting and buckling. Buildings were toppling against and through one another as the shockwave rippled out from its impact point.

As the Marineers dropped, scrambled and skidded down though the rotting and rusted sub-levels, with passages and reinforced chambers collapsing about them, Allegra and Commander Tyrhone corrected their course. Allegra had a natural feel for the underhive environs of her youth, whereas Tyrhone used as his guiding star the signature traces recorded by his hand-held auspex.

Countless levels down and with the partially demolished colony settling dangerously above them, Allegra and the Marineers reached what they thought to be the rust-water-flooded bottom. The captain felt bedrock beneath her boots. Several of the Elites had activated their lamps and followed their commander as he in turn followed the insistence of the auspex through the knee-deep brown waters.

As the auspex delivered its final verdict, Tyrhone stopped and looked to Allegra. The captain nodded. Kneeling down, the commander felt his way through the waters. Removing several fistfuls of rust-muck, Tyrhone's usually grim face broke with a moment of relief.

'Got it,' he said to himself. 'Get those lamps in here,' he ordered, but no amount of illumination was going to cut through the murky water.

'Just do it by touch, commander,' Allegra said.

Tyrhone grunted, before pulling back the sleeve on one arm to reveal silver ink on his ebony skin. The Imperial Army security passcodes for the munitions depot. 'Four-point perimeter,' Tyrhone ordered the Elites. 'We don't know who or what might have followed us down here.'

'Nothing could have got through that,' one of the Marineers replied, jabbing a thumb skywards.

'We did,' Allegra told him simply.

'Just do it,' Tyrhone ordered, beginning to punch the codes into the submerged and chunky glyph-grid.

It took several attempts to input the codes. Whether the commander mis-struck a glyph stud or the water-infiltrated and antiquated hatch-mechanism didn't recognise the code was anyone's guess. As the hatch finally popped, rust-water started pouring down through the opening. With several of his Marineers, Tyrhone managed to get the hatch fully open.

'You four remain here,' he ordered the perimeter Elites. 'This is a maximum-security depot: nothing gets in. Do you understand?'

'Yes, commander,' the Marineers returned.

The munitions depot stank of rust and old air. It felt like a place of death. Climbing down the access ladder into the darkness, Allegra could almost hear the echo of old hatreds. Enmities of an older age: detestations strong enough to make forces want to inflict weapons of absolute destruction on one another. The kinds of weapons the depot had been built to house.

With rust-water still pouring in from above and pooling about their boots, Lux Allegra and the Marineer Elites stood at the bottom of the chamber. Amongst the servo-cranes and pulley-systems, orbital torpedoes and biological weapons sat in their cradles and carriers. Even through the flaking paint and rusted casings, the ominous glyphs and symbols still visible on their sides made it clear which of the munitions were weapons-exterminatus.

Taking pride of place at the heart of the chamber and keeping court in a dank palace of doom and destruction, the contingency force located the object of their mission. Three fat virus bombs sat there – rusted, forgotten and unrealised of purpose. As the Elites set lamp beams and eyes on the life-eaters, splashing footfalls became light and voices became hushed. Allegra and the Marineers stood and stared at the virus bombs. Dark moments passed.

Allegra took a deep breath of stale, corroded air.

'Master-vox,' she ordered. The Elite assigned to hump the comms-unit slipped its weight off his back and handed it to her. Settling it on a nearby torpedo, Allegra set the frequency.

'*Tiamat*, this is *Elite-One*, come in.'

The vox-static howled around the darkness of the depot. '*Elite-One* to *Tiamat*, passcode Kappa, Theta, Iota. This is a command priority, please respond.'

As the cold loneliness of the unanswered vox-request crept through the bones of the Marineers, Commander Tyrhone looked to Allegra for orders. She passed the hailer back to the vox-operator. 'Keep trying,' she told him, before turning back to Tyrhone.

'Let's get to work, commander,' Allegra ordered. Slipping his demolitions pack off one shoulder, the Marineer officer knelt down in the rising water before the first bomb and set to priming the life-eater for a launchless detonation.

SEVENTEEN

Eidolica – Alcazar Astra

'First Captain Garthas is dead, my lord.'

'Say again, oratorium, say again.'

With the mega-bolters and gatling blasters back to their raucous cacophony and the gunship *Escorchier* hovering above the void ramparts like a thunderous guardian angel, Captain Maximus Thane couldn't make Brother Zerberyn out.

'First Captain Garthas is dead,' the honorarius repeated solemnly across the private vox-channel.

Maximus Thane heard the words but it took a moment to process them.

'How?' was all he could think to say.

'Fortress-Monastery North pict captures record the First Captain's victory over the invaders' breach force,' Zerberyn reported.

'Yes, brother.'

'Lord Garthas was inspecting the dead and voxing new orders for Captain Xontague and his Fists,' the Honour

Guard Space Marine said. 'One of the savages – a boarder, a hull breacher – still breathed in the First Captain's presence. It was alive when its injuries dictated it should not be.'

'Continue, Brother Zerberyn.'

'It detonated the hull-cracking breach charge it carried, taking Lord Garthas and his honour guard with it,' the honorarius said. 'Their plate could not protect them from such a charge. Lord Garthas was found, but the Chief Apothecary said he could not be saved.'

Thane stared bitterly out across the churning ocean of greenskin savagery that continued to roll up across the shattered void plating of the *Alcazar Astra*. Despite a full Eidolican night of fighting, despite the taking of life in ghastly swathes and the mettle of Dorn's sons being put sorely to the test, the green invader came still. The attack moon had blanket-bombed the Eidolican dark side with rocks and crash transports. Hulks and landers still rocketed into the black desert-world dunes, vomiting forth alien barbarians – their brief thunderbolt transit rattling and shaking them into a bottomless fury. No matter how many enemy lives the Fists Exemplar took in the name of their dead Chapter Masters and primarch, the ork attack moon supplied more.

Master Aloysian had been as good as his word. Despite his doubts, the Master of the Forge had used his skills and prayers to bring the star fort's only operational plasma drive to explosive life. The mighty engine column, that as one of four would have helped transport and manoeuvre the mighty *Alcazar Astra* in-system, blasted the fortress-monastery from its sandy foundations, turning the black desert to obsidian about it. As Master Aloysian had faithfully predicted, the star fort did not ascend. It inclined.

Rising on the Transept East engine column, everything not mag-locked to the gore-slick void plating began to slip and tumble away. Fifth Captain Tyrian watched as thousands of greenskin savages fell away from the edge of the void hull and down into the plasma-drive-roasted sands. Creatures skidded and slid towards the company's chain-blades and boltguns, allowing the Adeptus Astartes to end them with ease. With their boots firmly locked to the metal deck, Xontague, captain of the Eighth, and his company cut through the monstrosities roaring and clawing uselessly past them. Captain Kastril and his Scout Marines secured themselves to the gargoylesque architecture of Fortress-Monastery North. When the deck began to rumble and tilt, the scouts picked off beasts from the plummeting masses with their sniper rifles over the pauldrons of their Ninth Company brothers.

For Thane and the Second Company, the sea of green receded at the captain's command. One moment Thane and Apothecary Reoch were back-to-back, carving and blasting pieces off gargantuan alien thugs; the next the deck was empty but for the dripping statues of Fists Exemplar, splattered in alien gore and mag-locked to the inclining deck. Monsters scraped, scrambled and scratched at the hull plating and each other, furious that gravity should drag them away from their quarry. Claws and weapons failed to provide purchase when sunk into the blood-smeared armour plating, and those monsters desperate and fast enough to grab something and hold on were swiftly blasted from their ledges by nearby Space Marines. As soon as the guns on the void ramparts re-established their firing protocols and the Thunderhawks assumed a similar suppression role above the helmets of the Fists Exemplar, Thane ordered Master Aloysian to gently reduce thrust and allow the plasma engine to take them back to the sands.

The strategy had succeeded. Despite shattering the fortress-monastery's superstructure further and rending great rifts in its void plating and architecture, the star fort had been denied to the greenskin invader. Both Space Marines and deck guns were replenished with precious ammunition from the fort's armoury vaults and for the hours of darkness that followed, the innumerable invaders were kept at murderous ballistic range. Chapter serfs returned to the ramparts with ammunition and supplies, while Apothecary Reoch took the opportunity to down the chainblade that had wreaked such horrific wounds on others and look instead to the wounds that had been visited on his brothers by the enemy.

Hours passed. About the void deck perimeter a wall of greenskin carcasses steamed. Deck ordnance and gunships thundered. Boltguns blazed. Mist-banks of gore drifted through the desert darkness. The greenskin invaders died in their droves. They kept coming, however. Something primordial and predacious drew them across the dunes to their death. Hourly their numbers were replenished by new monsters, raining down on Eidolica in a shower of wanton conquest. Hulking creatures, fresh in their bestial rage, salivating through tusk-crowded maws and fixing the growing silhouette of the *Alcazar Astra* with their beady eyes.

The silhouette was growing because the Fists Exemplar and Second Captain Maximus Thane – ranking officer on the void ramparts and now ranking officer aboard the star fort itself – had reached their objective. The Eidolican dawn. The razorblade sliver of Frankenthal's Star – the system sun that had once threaten to swallow the fortress-monastery whole – was reaching over the distant western dunes.

Even with such a meagre shaft of intense light cutting across the skies, the Fists Exemplar home world was revealed. In the still air and black deserts of Eidolica, the eye travelled far. An Adeptus Astartes' sight travelled even further. Promethium wells raged at the heavens, belching black, oily smoke skywards. Little could be seen of the Eidolican black sands about the fortress-monastery. As far as a Space Marine could see, there were monsters. A sea of alien ferocity, swamping the deserted sands with their filthy presence. The dawn light drew a conqueror's roar from the beasts and the air trembled with their intention to bring slaughter to the star fort's defenders.

Further to the south, across the green sea of doom, rocks and hulks streaked into the promethium fields, thudding into the sands and killing their own – only for twice the number of dead to flood from the crude transits. Between swarms of junk landers descended larger greenskin droppers and tractor-tugs, all magna-grapnels, beam-anchors and rocket engines. These ungainly transports lacked the thunderbolt impatience of other crash transits. Instead they lowered colossal engines of war to the distant planet surface. Brute representations of greenskin gods and their Beast warlord, crafted from mountains of scrap and crude engineering.

His suit's auto-senses detected the breeze. Maximus Thane nodded to himself. The rising sun brought with it the movement of air.

'Companies,' Thane called across the open vox-channel. 'Conserve ammunition. Cease fire.'

The chatter of bolter fire died on the wind, swiftly followed by the accompanying boom of Thunderhawk guns and deck ordnance. No longer held back by a wall of skull-shattering bolt-rounds, the greenskins clawed their way over their dead and thundered up the void deck to meet their enemy. Their blades glinted dully, rude and unblooded. Their weaponry crashed wildly at the defenders, showering the deck with sparks and ricochets. Their tusks parted and raucous calls of pure animal aggression built to a rising crescendo in their barrel chests. The ramparts trembled with their bootfalls.

With boltguns silent about them, the Fists Exemplar stared down their hated enemy. No gauntlet grabbed for sword or pistol. No battle-brother moved from his position on the armoured hull. The invader drew close. The wild fire from their guns drew closer. Axes, mauling blades and chain-choppers came up. The monsters dribbled like mongrels at the expectation of brutality and violence, barbarically realised. Three thunderous strides away. Two. One.

The tentative twilight of dawn was no more. Great shafts of sunlight erupted over the horizon. Eidolica had turned. Day had broken on the desert world. Night – usually a time of industriousness and mass production across the promethium fields and worksteads – had turned to glorious day. Usually the radiance harvesters and photovoltaic enclosures would take over, harnessing the benefits of Eidolica's proximity to its parent star. They now sat in shattered, silvery shards on the black desert sands in the wake of the greenskin hordes.

The sun rose. The dunes about the *Alcazar Astra* stood naked before the intense heat and radiation of Frankenthal's Star. The temperature leapt and the sands were baked black in thermonuclear brilliance. The desert world turned, leaving the attack moon behind, and the system sun began its ascendency – its dominion absolute in the Eidolican skies. Maximus Thane's helmet optics introduced filters to protect the captain's engineered eyes. Everything became brilliant and white. The enemy hordes became as one. A jagged silhouette. A black wall against the brightness, all tusks, spiked armour and serrated weaponry.

First there was flame. Anything combustible on the invaders' bodies – rudimentary clothing, decorative skins and heavy leathers – burned. The intense radiation roasted their tough flesh to charcoal and cooked through their organs. By the time Frankenthal's Star had done with them and the greenskin beasts reached Maximus Thane and his Fists Exemplar battle line, they were no more than soot and ash, carried away on the breeze.

The Adeptus Astartes stood out on the void ramparts for a few moments longer, their paintless plate seared in the lightstorm to a chromatic burnishment.

'Companies,' Thane called across the vox-channel. 'To the fortress-monastery.'

The silhouettes and shadows of statuesque Space Marines turned in the still inferno. They stomped through the blinding brightness back to their bays, hangars and barbican-locks, where Thane ordered the star fort's blast shields down. Great metal shields and defences – that would have been used against the green invader had the situation made it necessary – closed, protecting the *Alcazar Astra*'s openings and observation ports from the radiation and roasting indifference of Frankenthal's Star during the deadly Eidolican day.

With the star fort's shields down and carrying the burden of a full night's battle and bloodshed, it would have been tempting for the Fists Exemplar to return to their cells for rest and cult observances. But there was simply too much to do. The fortress-monastery had taken a battering, and it would take more than the full day of radiant preservation they had to repair and fortify it in readiness for the fresh and endless onslaught of enemy forces the next night. On the Eidolican nightside, Seventh Captain Dentor still fought the enemy on the Tharkis Flats. During the stellar disruption of daytime, vox-transmissions were not possible, but Maximus Thane trusted that Dentor would take refuge in the sub-steads and ancient cave networks of the Great Basin, waiting out the enemy as they roasted in the rolling Eidolican dawn.

As the captain and Mendel Reoch strode through the launch bays, between the anchored Thunderhawks, Thane turned to his Apothecary.

'I give thanks for you, brother,' Thane told Reoch. 'Thanks for your nerve and tenacity; thanks for your good counsel,' the captain managed a half-smile, 'and mostly thanks for the skill of that damned sword arm.'

Reoch paused and looked to his captain and friend. With

a vox-grille for a mouth, the Apothecary had no smile to return. It was plain he struggled with such appreciation.

'I give thanks for the dawn,' Reoch said. 'I suspect I'll be needed in the apothecarion.' As the launch bay blast doors boomed to a close behind them, Reoch peeled off to the left. 'You, Master Thane, will be needed in the tactical oratorium.'

'I'm not Chapter Master,' Maximus Thane said. The captain was superstitious about such things but, with Alameda and Garthas dead, he was next in the chain of command.

'Might as well be,' Reoch said. 'With or without the title, the burden of responsibility is just the same.'

Thane found Honorarius Zerberyn in the oratorium. The Fist Exemplar was a mess of rent armour, dressings and stapled wounds. He had bled over the oratorium floor, which a serf was addressing with mop and bucket.

'Captain,' Zerberyn greeted him. Thane pursed his lips.

'We have not always seen eye to eye,' Thane said finally.

'Captain?'

'I have had cause at times to deem you officious, lacking in humility and overly ambitious,' the captain said. The Honour Guard Space Marine's eyes fell. 'But you are capable and served both Master Alameda and the First Captain well. And as ranking Adeptus Astartes, I will have sore need of you also. Would you consent to remain on as my honorarius – for the Fists Exemplar now have but one – and the emissary of my intentions?'

Zerberyn, whose features were used to hiding some petty notion or unspoken grievance, simply gave the captain a nod of respect and reassurance.

'It would be my honour to serve you, sir, in whatever way I can.'

'Thank you, brother,' Thane said. 'Would you begin by asking the Chaplain to attend me in Master Alameda's chambers, I shall need his guidance. Then assemble both the fortress masters and company captains here in the tactical oratorium. Summon Sergeant Anatoq in place of Captain Hieronimax. Sergeant Hoque for the Second Company. I shall need a status report from the Chief Apothecary on the number of dead and wounded as soon as possible – and also have the Chapter Standard Bearer report to me.'

'Brother Byzander is dead, my lord,' Zerberyn informed him.

Thane nodded. 'I'm sorry for that,' the captain said. 'Send for my own bearer Brother Aquino, in his stead.'

'Right away, sir.'

'Then get yourself to Apothecary Reoch, to address your injuries,' Thane ordered the Space Marine. 'If he is half as good at closing wounds as opening them, you should be in good hands.'

EIGHTEEN

Terra – Mount Vengeance

Drakan Vangorich took his throne in the crypt-nexus. The temple operations chamber was dark. About the Grand Master were a select gathering of tacticians, sans-expediens, infocytes, temple alternals and officio logistas – but he wouldn't have known it, for all the evidence of their presence. In the blackness, the Grand Master's operational staff and advisors were just disembodied voices, echoing about the chamber.

'Initiate,' Vangorich commanded.

The darkness flickered to life as the crypt-nexus became the projected site of a chamber-spanning hololithic representation. The three-dimensional image was crisp and rich in colour and texture, but portrayed a first person perspective.

'I can see what he is seeing,' Vangorich said, 'but can he hear what I am saying?'

'I am receiving you, Grand Master,' came the deep voice of Esad Wire – the Officio operative better known to his fellows

as Beast. With any good fortune, the crypt-nexus was about to witness some of Beast's talents at work – relayed directly from the holoptometric implants behind Esad Wire's cruel eyes.

'Assassin,' Drakan Vangorich told his living weapon, 'you are mission affirmative. Do me proud, Beast Krule.'

Esad Wire cast his gaze at the ground. He was in a wardroom. Starched Naval uniforms hung about lockers and stands, while the bodies they were supposed to adorn decorated the wardroom floor. Officers and ensigns of the First Royal Provost's Naval Security Battalion had lost their lives in the discovery of an onboard imposter in their wardroom. Beast Krule had made light work of the Naval security armsmen, breaking bones and backs as he swiftly dealt with his discoverers. Sealing off the bulkhead hatch, the Assassin proceeded to select an armsman's uniform to cram his muscular bulk into and completed the disguise with a ceremonial lasquebus, a monomolecular-edged sabre and Scipio-pattern pistol.

The ridiculous Naval foppery of his uniform complete, Beast Krule had crushed the bodies into a wardroom ablutory. Closing the cubicle door, he allowed the weight of the bodies against it to provide sufficient deterrent to weak-bladdered ensigns or armsmen curious at the disappearance of their comrades. By the time they were actually discovered, Krule planned on being long gone. Pulling the strap about his chin and the visor down on his broad-top cap, the Assassin left the wardroom and strode out into an ante-corridor.

Making his steps strident, his back straight and his boots squeak in time with a group of similarly dressed Royal

Provost's men, Krule marched out onto the hangar deck of the Emperor-class battleship *Autocephalax Eternal.* The hangar housed lines of gleaming starfighters and battalion presentations of what Beast Krule estimated to be two or three thousand armsmen. Like him they were ceremonially dressed and presenting arms in the form of honour-guard lasquebuses. Many were already gathered in tight at-ease formations before the podium and vox-casters at the end of the hangar. Many more were still marching in to take their positions.

The march was long and dull as the contingent Beast had attached himself to made their way up the length of the rally gathering. Out of the hangar the Assassin could see the byzantine insanity of Ancient Terra slowly turning. The *Autocephalax Eternal* was stationed in low orbit, flanked by her own ceremonial escort of ancient heavy frigates, hanging like ornate baubles above the hive-world.

As Beast Krule drew closer to the podium, he went through the simple rituals of his deadly craft. He checked the tools of his trade. The weapons in his possession were next to useless. Both the lasquebus and the Scipio pistol were empty of power pack and ammunition. In the presence of such an important personage, the chance of an accidental weapons discharge – especially under the extra pressure of the ceremonial occasion – could not be tolerated.

That had been part of the genius of it. Surrounded by thousands of armsmen, the target might well feel safe and let his guard down. Not a single ensign, officer or member of the Royal Provost's, however, carried live ammunition. This had made the time and location of the operation tempting.

The monomolecular sabre was more of a hacking and slashing weapon: a thug's blade, for all its craft and finery.

Nothing would give Krule the split-second, single-action kill that was required of the situation better than his own tools: the rippling muscles of his murderer's arms and the heavy-gauge, plasteel-infused bones of his hands. When formed into fists, the deadweight of the durable metal, propelled by his bulging arms, crashed with ease through skulls and rib cages. When ordinary men pummelled one another, the pair walked away with bruises and bloodied lips. When Beast Krule beat a target to death – his favoured mode of execution and the reason for his brutal moniker – bone shattered, organs were torn free and heads were knocked clean off. Coupled with an expert knowledge of physiology and multiple hand-to-hand combat proficiencies, Beast's hands had known little idleness in his early service to the Officio Assassinorum.

The Assassin could hear his target clearly now. He was close enough to be in range of the podium vox-hailers. Many of his contingent had found their places in the neatly formed lines of armsmen before the podium, but Beast walked on up the central thoroughfare, his visor down and both march and stance impeccable.

'...and so I am delighted to order Admiral Villiers and the fighting men and women of the *Autocephalax Eternal* to the Glaucasian Gulf,' Lord High Admiral Lansung boomed, 'to assume command of the Armada Segmenta, gathering above Lepidus Prime at my command.'

The Lord High Admiral was the very definition of an easy target. Huge in his acres of Naval blue uniform, his red face told of an extended lifetime working out of luxurious cabins, enjoying fine fortified wines and the lavish offerings of a private galley. He looked like he had never drawn a pistol or hanger in his life, having the family and political connections to command without ever having to do so. His sheer bulk meant that during an attempted escape he wouldn't get far and it wasn't as though his security detail of Lucifer Blacks – further from him than usual in the apparent safety of the Naval rally – could lift him and rush him to a shuttle with any great haste.

At his side was an equally feeble specimen of a man. Like Lansung he had enjoyed all of the benefits of a Naval officer's existence and none of the hardships. Admiral Sheridan Villiers, His Grace the Void Baron of Cypra Nubrea, had a face that reminded Krule of a horse and a laryngeal prominence in his throat the size of a small asteroid.

Beast Krule felt his pace quicken. He was closing. He was close. The smaller details of his disguise were no longer needed. He was still just an armsman finding his place at the front of the rally congregation. He could taste blood. He could feel the crack of bones.

The quick march turned into a run. Lansung was still talking. He was handing over to the *Autocephalax Eternal*'s gawkish commanding officer. Krule dropped his lasquebus and with a flick of a finger, unbuckled his belt and holster. Carrying the holster, scabbard, pistol and sabre with it, the belt *thunked* to the deck. Beast Krule was on the steps, his storming strides taking him up two or three at a time. Some alarm had now become evident in the audience. Still confused at the bizarre actions of one of their own, the

ROB SANDERS

armsmen simply stared. Villiers' brow had registered his displeasure – it was his battleship and security battalions on show, after all.

Lansung, however, betrayed the slowly dawning suspicion that he was in trouble. Krule saw the High Lord's eyes widen and the arteries in his neck constrict. His security detail were finally on the move. Lucifer Blacks raced from adjoining corridors and cavities in the bay walls. They were too far away, however. Beast Krule had his quarry. The Assassin, his defenceless prey.

Krule's cap and visor fell away as he leapt from the top step up onto the podium. Villiers had made some attempt to go for his hanger but was struggling to get it clear of its scabbard. The Assassin fancied that with so little use but so much polish, the blade was stuck. Lansung backed away. There was no going for a blade for him. Horror sat simply on the Lord High Admiral's broad face.

With a bound, Beast Krule leapt from the podium at Lansung. Like a predatory feline, Krule cleared Villiers and landed on the small island of fat flesh that was Admiral Lansung. Lansung crashed heavily to the deck. Beast Krule was on top of him. Boots in his sides. Knees in his mountainous chest. One murderous hand clutched a globed shoulder, while the other retracted in a hefty fist. The Assassin was spoiled for choice. Where to punch his plasteel-infused knuckles? Through the Admiral's triple chins and through his spine? Through his ribcage to splatter his meaty heart? No, the Assassin decided. He would smash through the High Lord's fat skull and mash the ambitions of a dangerous mind into the deck.

Beast Krule suddenly saw a collection of panic-strewn words spill from Lansung's patrician lips. They were called as an order to those about him. To the closing Lucifer Blacks. To his flag staff. To Villiers and the officers of the *Autocephalax Eternal.* The Assassin sensed the importance of the order and somehow found his way back to the moment.

'Firing protocol thirteen!' the Lord High Admiral screamed. 'For Throne's sake: firing protocol thirteen!'

No more words, Beast Krule decided. The fist came down.

'Hold!' Drakan Vangorich called.

Obedience. Krule turned his fist aside, smashing its metallic force into the hangar deck.

'What in damnation is "Firing protocol thirteen"?' the Grand Master demanded.

The hololithic representation sizzled to darkness and from that darkness temple infocytes, sans-expediens and tacticians came forwards in deference. A wall section started to shudder to one side, revealing a small chamber in a lighter shade of twilight beyond. Esad Wire was strapped to a simulcra slab. His temple-crafted body was needled from head to toe with sensors. Lines ran into impulse links in the side of his skull and fibre threads into the flesh between his ears and eyes, interfacing with the holoptometric implants beyond.

The Assassin sat up, tearing the sensor needles and datalines from his body. The indoctranostic holosimulation was over. The frustration was clear on Wire's face. The predator had not taken down his prey. He had failed in some way. His temple re-education – his murderous strategic orientation – had been halted by a furious Drakan Vangorich.

'Again,' Vangorich said, 'what is this "Firing protocol thirteen"? That's new. I haven't heard of that.'

'It's a proxy,' an infocyte volunteered. 'Officio operatives aboard the battleship gave us the physical detailing. It's not a recovered piece of intelligence. It's a proxy created by the strategium.'

'A proxy for what?' Vangorich demanded.

A hooded tactician came forwards.

'The hypothetical came out of the logistuary,' the tactician said. She swiftly added, 'Operative Wire's encounter with an Inquisitorial tail at Tashkent factored in a greater range of eventualities for the logistas. Firing protocol thirteen is a proxy for a target behaviour based on logical extensions of those eventualities.'

'Like?' Vangorich said dangerously.

'The knowedge of certain Officio Assassinorum installations and their locations,' the tactician told him, 'by involved and interconnected factions.'

'Covert temple facilities?'

'Such delicate information could be traded between numerous individuals and organisations – the Holy Inquisition, the Ecclesiarchy, the Adeptus Mechanicus, the Imperial Navy...'

'So firing protocol thirteen in this context could be?' Vangorich pressed.

'The location of the Mount Vengeance Officio Assassinorum facility,' the tactician told him.

'Knowledge of this facility?' Vangorich confirmed, briefly casting his gaze at a wounded-looking Wire.

'It's on a list of five possibilities,' the tactician said. 'The target's behaviour would facilitate a stalemate scenario. The operative would be powerless to execute his mission with the target in possession of such information. If he attempted to do so, the battleship in the simulated scenario would fire its guns from orbit on this location. We have calculated, however, that the true nature of both the weapon's discharge and the temple location would remain secret. The incident would be recorded as a regrettable accident.'

'Well that's a relief,' Vangorich said sardonically. The import was lost on the tactician. The Grand Master was out of his throne and walking towards the egress-archway. He stopped and turned to the gathered temple staff. 'I want this facility cleared of temple personnel, intelligence and equipment within the hour.'

'Yes, Grand Master.'

'Enough with simulations. Beast Krule,' Vangorich said, 'with me.'

Having removed the last of the impulse jacks from his head and the sensor needles from his flesh, Esad Wire followed his master out of the crypt-nexus.

'What are we going to do?' Esad Wire said.

'We're going to force the Lord High Admiral's hand,' Vangorich told him. 'Gathering an armada in the Glaucasian Gulf will do nothing to protect the core systems from the xenos threat. What I wouldn't give for a stalemate scenario out there.'

'Where are we going?' Esad Wire asked.

'Somewhere the admiral's great guns can't reach us,' Vangorich told his Assassin.

NINETEEN

Eidolica – Alcazar Astra

The company chapel was empty. That was the way Maximus Thane preferred it. His Fists Exemplar – from his captains and masters, to his battle-brothers and their Chapter serfs – were all were too busy with preparations for dusk. Thane's desperate strategy had saved many Space Marine lives but had cost the *Alcazar Astra* dearly. Splits and rents in the thick plate of the void ramparts were only the beginning. The star fort had suffered serious structural damage and the generatorium had also experienced damage-inflicted failings. As ranking Adeptus Astartes aboard the star fort, however, it wasn't Thane's job to repair ceramite, replenish ammunition or audit the armoury. It wasn't even his direct responsibility now to ensure that others performed those essential roles – he had given Sergeant Hoque temporary command of the Second Company.

It was Thane's function to decide which strategy would best ensure the survival of Eidolica. Which strategy would inflict greatest damage on the invader. Which strategy – if any – could possibly combine both.

Even the Second Company's chapel hadn't escaped the damage and desolation. Without the artificial gravity and inertial dampeners that the star fort would have benefited from in the void, the chapel – like every other hallowed chamber in the fortress-monastery – had been turned almost on its side. Minor Chapter relics lay smashed on the floor about their cases. Statues had toppled and tapestries had fallen across the altar. Placing his helmet to one side, Thane cleared up as best he could.

Thane's favourite artefact – one of the reasons he frequented the tiny chapel as much as he did – had also been damaged. Set in a shallow central column, between the altar and the narrow entrance archway, was a small stained-glass window. It depicted Rogal Dorn – not in battle or during the desperation of the Great Heresy, but at deliberation. The window pictured Dorn deep in thought, still clad in his golden armour.

It was the moment Dorn decided to break up his beloved Legion and embrace the Codex Astartes, creating numerous successor Chapters from his stalwart and loyal Imperial Fists. Thane loved the window not least because the Fists Exemplar had been created in that moment. Like all of the Imperial Fists Second Founding Chapters, their character came from the individuals making up their ranks. The Chapter crusaders and zealots gravitated to Sigismund, while to Alexis Polux went the younger, more impressionable brothers. Many of the attrition fighters that would make up the Excoriators had held the Palace walls during the siege of Terra and had found brotherhood with Demetrius Katafalque.

It was well known that the primarch and his genetic sons struggled with the decision to break up their Legion. There were some, however, that came around to Guilliman's wisdom – as Dorn himself did at last – swifter than others. Captain Oriax Dantalion had spoken for the sense and necessity of such drastic action among the Imperial Fists early in the process. This had initially earned Dorn's disappointment, and some said enmity. When Dorn himself searched his soul and reached the conclusion that the window illustrated, he remembered Dantalion's earlier wisdom. He rewarded the captain with a Chapter of his own – made up of progressive battle-brothers not unlike himself. They were deemed exemplars of the new order, and named the Fists Exemplar by the primarch.

Looking at the window, Thane discovered that some of the fragile glass pieces had fallen free of their leadwork. Dorn's depiction was now marred with hollows and missing sections. Many of the pieces had smashed on the flags of the small chapel during the firing of the engine column. Thane discovered, however, that one piece had survived intact. A section of yellow glass, representing a piece of the primarch's sacred, golden plate. Picking it up and turning it about in the tips of his gauntlets, Thane slipped it delicately back into place.

As the archway door rose beyond, light from the corridor lamps blazed through the window. The illuminated window, bringing Rogal Dorn's depiction to dazzling radiance, held Maximus Thane's attention – so much so that he hardly noticed Brother Zerberyn enter the company chapel.

'My lord,' Zerberyn said, taking to his knee before the altar and kissing the ceramite knuckles of his gauntleted fist one after another.

'Brother?'

'My lord,' Zerberyn said, getting up, 'sentries report a strange disturbance at the east barbican lock.'

'What kind of disturbance?'

'Impacts on the outer doors,' Zerberyn said, 'like something trying to get in.'

'No greenskin survives the attentions of Frankenthal's Star,' Thane averred.

'The alien invader is much invested in terrible new technologies,' the honorarius said. Thane nodded.

'Have Sergeant Hoque meet me at the barbican with a squad,' Thane said. 'Then lock off the section interior bulkheads surrounding the barbican. If it is the invader, we'll see to it that he won't get far.'

'Very good, my lord,' Zerberyn said, and left Maximus Thane alone with Dorn once again.

Taking up his helmet and setting off for the East Transept, the captain encountered Sergeant Hoque en route past the company chapel. He marched with Hoque and his squad down to the barbican lock.

'Opinion, brother?' Thane put to Gaspar, the sentry whose post the barbican had been.

'Sounded too measured and deliberate for the greenskins, sir,' Gaspar said, but his boltgun was still aimed at the barbican portal. Thane waited. Behind them, the section bulkhead hatches began to lower.

Then they heard it. The sound of something smashing a great fist against the thick metal door. It didn't sound like a rabid savage or alien invader.

'Sergeant,' Thane said, prompting Hoque and his men to form a gauntlet of gaping barrels in the barbican chamber. If their visitor was indeed hostile, Hoque and his men would ensure that its welcome would be brief. Thane put on his battle-helm. 'Brother Gaspar, if you will.'

The sentry fired the airlock mechanism and the massive door began to rumble towards the ceiling. Blinding Eidolican daylight seared its way under the door and began to fill the barbican, prompting the auto-senses of the captain's plate to respond and initiate optical filters.

As the portal shuddered open and the Fists Exemplar leant into their boltguns, a single silhouette appeared at the door. A black shape in a power-armoured suit waited for them. As the boltgun barrels lowered, the Adeptus Astartes framed in the blinding light of the doorway stepped inside. He was swiftly joined by several other battle-brothers in sealed plate.

'Lower it,' Thane commanded Brother Gaspar. As the armoured door lowered and the barbican turned to darkness, the filter optics of Thane's helmet returned to normal spectra. Not fast enough for the captain, however, who promptly removed his helmet.

Before him stood a crusade marshal in the roasted midnight plate of the Black Templars. A skull-helmed Chaplain

stood to his side, while two Sword Brethren flanked the pair with their power swords and crusader shields. The final member of the group was a Fists Exemplar captain, clad in the temperature-tarnished bare ceramite of the Chapter. As the captain took off his helm, Thane could see that it was Dentor of the Seventh.

'It's a relief to see you, captain,' Thane told him.

'Likewise, Maximus,' Dentor replied.

As the Black Templars commander relieved himself of his burning helm, Dentor introduced him. 'Captain Thane, this is Marshal Bohemond of the Vulpius Crusade.'

'An honour, brother-captain,' Bohemond offered.

'Likewise, marshal,' Thane said, 'and a surprise: we sent out broad-range requests for fraternal assistance, but did not think you so close. You are, of course, warmly welcome to *Alcazar Astra* and a share of the honour to come. How many battle-brothers do you have at your command, marshal?'

Bohemond's eyes were hard but understanding. He seemed to nod to himself.

'Second captain,' Dentor said, 'the Marshal does not...'

'Thank you, captain,' Bohemond said, cutting him off. 'You are ranking Adeptus Astartes here?'

'I am.'

'I wonder if we might speak alone, sir?' The Black Templar's eyes never left his Fists Exemplar opposite.

'Of course, marshal,' Thane said. 'I know just the place.'

With the barbican re-secured and Bohemond's men entertained, Thane led the Black Templar Marshal into the company chapel. It was closer than the oratorium and, with the daylight hours filled with repair and industry, still deserted. Bohemond fixed upon the stained glass representation of Dorn immediately. Falling down to his knees, he hammered his armoured fist into his breastplate at the four points of the crusader cross.

'Beautiful,' Bohemond said as he got back up.

'Marshal,' Maximus Thane said, staring across the altar, 'I do not wish to break with ritual or tradition but my world turns. With night comes the enemy and an opportunity to avenge our fallen.'

'I've seen your world,' Bohemond said, 'and the xenos attack moon hanging over it. Your black sands swarm with orks. They travel with the terminator. In their cunning they have become wise to your planet's lethalities. Tomorrow, the enemy takes this fortress: from orbit it is plain to see.'

'It is not as simple as that.'

'Captain, it is every bit as simple as that,' Bohemond told him.

'I expected more from Sigismund's crusaders,' Thane told him. 'It does not become a Templar to turn his cheek from the fight. You speak of odds. What are odds to a son of Dorn?'

'It smarts, doesn't it, captain?' the Black Templar said as he wandered about the chapel. 'I should know. You're right: it does not become us. But our cheek is not turned. We are simply facing the other way. We are crusaders, and crusades are not won on single days or single worlds. And that is all Eidolica is: a single world with a single day.'

'You speak cavalierly about our prospects, marshal,' Thane said. 'Why don't you help us improve them?'

'I already have,' Bohemond replied. 'My Thunderhawks pulled Captain Dentor and what was left of his company from the greenskin-drenched wilderness.'

'You had no right, Templar,' Thane spat.

'They would be dead now if I hadn't.'

'And what of the populations they were protecting? What is to become of them?'

'Nothing, captain,' Bohemond said, 'for they are dead already.'

'I need your men, Bohemond.'

'You can't have them,' the Marshal said. 'For they are needed elsewhere – as are yours, captain.'

'Marshal...'

'I have been where you are now,' the Black Templar told him. 'It is not easy for an Adeptus Astartes to turn and run, but as my castellan told me, it is merely a matter of perspective. There is running from and there is running to. We were at Aspiria, and yes, I could have sent my Templars to their deaths in the name of obstinacy and honour. But then I heard the call – as you hear now. Dorn's call. I heard it in Imperial Navy recalls, in my battle-barge's klaxons, in mortis-cries echoing across the immaterium. The call home, brother. Coreward.'

'You are a crusader,' Thane accused. 'You call no world home. Eidolica is home to the Fists Exemplar.'

Bohemond smashed his fist against the plate of his chest.

'No,' the marshal hissed, 'this is your home. You say your Eidolica needs you. I say your Imperium needs you. Do you have any idea how many astropathic calls for assistance I had to ignore to reach you, brother? Worlds die about us and sectors fall. This is not localised. The invader has not a conqueror's eyes for your piecemeal world, captain. Eidolica is an afterthought – the enemy's bloody gaze is fixed on the segmentum whole. What good can you do here?'

'This is my world,' Maximus Thane roared through the window at the marshal. 'These are my people. This is my bastion.'

'Your people are finished,' Bohemond told him. He let the cold sentiment hang in the descending silence of the chapel. 'Through no fault of your own or your commanders', your world belongs to savages of the void. This was never a battle you could win. How long can you keep this up: fighting through the night and hiding in the light? How long will your armouries sustain you? A day? A week? And should you slaughter every living greenskin on the surface of your desert world, what then? The xenos attack moon will tear this tiny planet apart and feed it to its guardian star.'

'What would you have me do?'

'I would have you do nothing, captain. What *we* must do – brothers all – is gather our strength. The savages will be stopped here no more than they would have been at Aspiria. We must consult with Chapter Master Mirhen; with my own High Marshal; with Scharn; with Quesadra of the Crimson Fists and Issachar of the Excoriators. It is time for the scattered successors of all loyal Legions to join once again in defence of humanity. This will not happen here, Thane; it will not happen now. But we must be as one and ready for Dorn's call, when it comes.'

Maximus Thane hadn't been looking at Bohemond for a while. His eyes were fixed on his primarch, picked out

in coloured glass. Neither battle-brother spoke for what seemed like a long time.

'Look, Thane,' Bohemond said. 'I speak like a brother of wisdom, when I learned this just like you, in the fires of battle. I found this decision no less difficult or painful.'

'Your vessels wait ready in orbit?' the Fist Exemplar asked.

'Yes,' the marshal replied. 'They hold position in the sun-blind. My gunships could have your brothers and materiel evacuated within the hour.'

Thane didn't need to check with a chronometer. Night was coming. He could feel the seconds ebbing away.

'Well, an hour is about all we have,' he said. Bohemond nodded his understanding.

The Fists Exemplar captain and the marshal went to leave the chapel. At the archway bulkhead, Thane turned to take one last look at the stained glass window.

'You think that it hurt Dorn, to break his Legion thus?' Thane asked, his voice echoing about the company chapel.

'More than the most grievous of wounds received in battle,' Bohemond said gently. 'But sometimes, you have to destroy something old in order to make something new. The Fists Exemplar know that better than any of Dorn's sons.'

Maximus Thane nodded slowly in grave agreement.

TWENTY

Undine – Desolation Point

Drip. Drip. Drip.

The storage depot was slowly flooding with rust-water. Lux Allegra sat on top of one of the bulbous virus bombs. Every so often, Commander Tyrhone would wade over and crank the munitions cradle up another notch to keep both the life-eater and the priming demolition charge out of the rising water. The Marineer Elites were similarly sat astride or perched on the corroded torpedoes and ancient orbitals that were stored in the chamber. Many leant their lascarbines against the weapon casings and their chins against the carbines. Lamps cut through the murk of the deep depot and the soldiers listened to the distant rumble of Desolation Point coming down on top of them. The colony was collapsing. Perhaps another rock had struck the island. Perhaps the impact damage of the first was still being felt as building collapsed into building, bringing the haven down in an almighty mountain of smoking scrap. Perhaps the fires had a role to play.

Speculation was pointless, Commander Tyrhone had

reminded his men, but there was little better to do than listen to the thunder of topside collapses or the sharp static of the vox. At intervals, Tyrhone's vox-operator would attempt to raise the Marineer submersible *Tiamat* without success. The contingency force had been holding position in the depot for hours. In all likelihood the *Tiamat* had been sunk, the victim of some fighter-bomber deployed torpedo or greenskin diving sphere.

Allegra's hands reached down to the flak about her abdomen, as was her habit. She found herself thinking of Lyle Gohlandr. The nights they had spent together and the baby growing in her belly. Gohlandr had been short-service – his duty due to end in only a matter of months. He had planned to return to Hive Galatae, apply to the harbour master for a security detail, and work the container stacks as his father had. Allegra would have been censured for conduct unbecoming an officer, but would still have received her gravidity leave. After having the baby, she would have joined Gohlandr at Galatae and got lost in the system. Forged identicodes were easy to come by if, like Allegra, you knew where to look.

The fantasy she had allowed herself, curled up in her berth, seemed a world away now. Undine had all but fallen. Galatae itself had actually fallen, crashing straight into the chemical seas. Gohlandr was dead and Lux Allegra did not have a world to bring her child into. The ocean world of Undine would be, at best, a warzone. At worst, Allegra, her child and her hive-kin could look forward to brutal existences as a xenos conqueror's slaves. Such bottomless misery filled the captain that for a moment she thought that she had dissipated into the chamber gloom. Her thoughts turned to even darker considerations.

'Commander,' she called across the murk, shattering the silence. 'You have been briefed on these weapons, yes?'

Tyrhone nodded. 'What happens when we set this thing off?' the captain put to him, tapping on the virus bomb's rusty casing with her nail.

'Is this necessary?' Tyrhone returned.

'Let's call it an order, commander,' Lux Allegra said.

'They call it Exterminatus,' Tyrhone said. 'Typically the device is orbitally deployed. The priming charge on these should be enough to initiate detonation and release of the virus compound.'

'Continue,' Allegra said. 'What happens after detonation? I want to hear it.'

Tyrhone stared at her. 'The virus breaks down organic material – anything it comes into contact with – on a molecular level, and it breaks it down fast. Estimates based on observational records suggest complete planetary biological infestation in a matter of minutes. Everything rots. Everything is broken down and reduced to sludge. Nothing organic will survive. Rebreathers will disintegrate and the seals of armour and airlocks will fail.'

'It will be quick?'

'Yes, captain,' Tyrhone said. 'It will be quick. The swift release of resulting flammable gases will require but a spark to initiate a planet-wide firestorm.'

'The oceans?'

'Will boil away,' Tyrhone said. 'Undine will be left a dead rock. No oceans. No atmosphere. No hives. No hivers.'

'No alien invader,' Allegra added.

'All will perish,' the commander confirmed. 'There will be nothing left.'

Lux Allegra nodded. One of the Marineers whimpered behind his lascarbine. The others remained deathly silent.

'Why three, if only one is required to do it?'

'The orbitals are ancient,' Tyrhone said. 'The potency of any one bomb might be compromised. Three should ensure mission success.'

'Mission success...'

'Yes, captain.'

'Thank you, commander.'

The master-vox screeched.

Allegra's heart jumped in her chest. The Marineers sat bolt upright.

'*Elite-one*, receive.'

It was General Phifer.

The vox-operator went to respond but Commander Tyrhone snatched up the pack. Wading through the rust-water, he deposited it in front of the captain. Allegra took the vox-hailer.

'Recieving, *Tiamat*, this is *Elite-one* – proceed.'

'Captain...'

'Receiving, *Tiamat*: proceed.'

'Captain,' the general said, 'the regimental astropath has received immaterial confirmation.'

'Yes, sir.'

'The Adeptus Astartes are not coming, captain.'

Phifer's news felt like a lasbolt to the heart for each of the Marineers. There was another whimper. Some lowered heads. Others gave nods of grim acceptance.

'Received, *Tiamat*,' Allegra replied.

'You are authorised to enact contingency measures,' the general said. 'I repeat: this is General Phifer and I am commanding you... to initiate contingency measures.'

'Yes sir,' Allegra replied. 'Order received and understood.'

The Marineers stared at the master-vox.

'Know this,' Phifer told them. 'We are going to win this battle. The battle for Undine. The battle for our world.'

Lux Allegra nodded.

'But lose the war,' she said, before dropping the vox-hailer in the rising waters and turning off the master-vox.

Nobody in the storage depot spoke. A minute, perhaps two, passed in silence.

'Captain,' Tyrhone began.

'There are no words,' Lux Allegra told him, bringing her knees up. 'Only duty.'

Tyrhone gave her the slightest of acknowledgements. A bob of his head. The clenching of teeth and the tightness of his lips. As Allegra sat on top of the fat fuselage of the orbital virus bomb, the Marineer Elite commander reached forwards to set off the charge detonator.

Hugging her arms around her belly, Lux Allegra's last thoughts were once again for what might have been, rather than what was – because what was, was oblivion.

TWENTY-ONE

Incus Maximal / Malleus Mundi – Orbital

Magos Urquidex entered the medicae section of the survey brig's laboratorium. He passed Alpha Primus Orozko and two heavily-armed Collatorax sentinels on his way in. Artisan Trajectorae Van Auken was taking no chances with their guest.

Urquidex approached the small mountain of blood-dotted dressings standing amongst the mess of the cybernurgical theatre. The giant stood before the three recovered cocoons on their slabs. He was still, although the rasping passage of air through his multilung was raw and audible.

Urquidex stood to one side and adjusted several calibrates on the tracked and itinerant trolley-stand that followed the patient around like an obedient hound. Lines and tubes ran from the equipment and into the folds of the Space Marine's dressings and hooded salve-robe. The giant didn't acknowledge Urquidex.

'I apologise for this,' the magos biologis said. 'You were not meant to see your Chapter brethren in this way. The autopsies are complete. The wonder of their design and genetic working has been honoured as the work of the Omnissiah. Last rites have been issued by our magi concisus, but we cannot carry out the appropriate cult observances out here.'

'No one can,' the giant rumbled.

'They will be placed in methalon storage for the rest of the journey,' Urquidex said. 'There is the matter of their official identification; for our records, of course.'

The giant turned and looked briefly at the magos biologis. The wet sores, burns and radiation scarring that afflicted the Space Marine's face made him appear raw and unfinished. The Imperial Fist turned back to the cocoons on the slabs. 'Perhaps their plate designations might have meaning for...'

'Diluvias: wall-name, Zarathustra,' the Adeptus Astartes told him. Urquidex noted the designation on a data-slate. 'Xavian: wall-name, Tranquility. Tylanor: wall-name, Dolorous.'

The Space Marine paused, his roll call complete. 'They were found–?' he asked after a moment.

'Coordinates three, sixty-two, seventy-two, fourteen,' Urquidex reported helpfully. 'There had been such gravitational upheaval–'

'The world turned itself inside out,' the Imperial Fist said. 'Chrome. Greenskin. Adeptus Astartes. Buried alive in mid-battle like some xenoarchaeological find. I had fought. I had killed. I don't know for how long. I felt the land moving beneath my boots. A cliff face erupted before me. A tidal wave of rock, earth and bodies. My brothers were down. The ground had swallowed them. I thought the magos dead, also.'

Urquidex walked with the giant over to where Phaeton Laurentis lay on his tracked stretcher. His ruined mouth still rehearsed the formation of words that had no meaning. He dribbled and pawed at the air with his hands.

'I think your assessment all but accurate,' Urquidex said. 'His workings sustain his failing organics. His cogitae and systems are being downstreamed for useful data. The magi physic do not expect him to live.'

'Do what you can, magos,' the Imperial Fist said. 'I owe him my life.' The Space Marine took the end of a piece of dressing, hanging loose from one great hand, and used it to clean a blood spot from Phaeton Laurentis' brow.

'How did you come to be on the *Amkulon* derelict?' Urquidex said, 'if you don't mind me asking? My artisan-primus requests the knowledge for his report.'

'I was alone,' the Adeptus Astartes said, 'on a planet the enemy was ripping apart. No one was coming for me. You cannot fight a planet with your sword. You cannot stand against it in your plate. All I had was the teleport homer... And hope.'

'It worked?'

'Yes.'

'When it formerly had not.'

'Yes.'

'You were vectored?'

'To the *Amkulon*,' the Space Marine confirmed. 'But there was a delay – not perceptible in transit. My plate detected the anomaly. Time had passed.'

'My artisan-primus believes that when the xenos attack-moon cleared the system, the gravitic interference that had impeded guided vectoring was removed. Upon the removal of the affecting body, your transit became complete. It is true that Magos Laurentis alerted us to your life signs. If the attack moon had not interrupted your transit then you would have arrived upon the toxic derelict earlier. You would have succumbed to radiation trauma and there would not have been life signs to find.'

'What are you saying, magos?' the Space Marine said, leaving Laurentis and standing before the armourglass viewport set in the laboratorium wall. With the blast screens retracted, the viewport allowed light from the void into the chamber. 'That I am the victim of good fortune?'

'If I believed in such a thing as good fortune,' Urquidex said, 'and I don't, then I should say you are very much its beneficiary. You are the last of your kind.'

'That's right,' the Imperial Fist said. 'I am the last of my kind. What good fortune is there in that?'

The pair turned their attentions to the two destruction-smeared ice worlds below. Despite the smouldering forges and cataclysmic black clouds that besmirched their twin surfaces, their reflected light still managed to dazzle.

'Yours?' the Space Marine asked.

'No longer,' Magos Urquidex said. 'But they are forge-worlds, lost to the xenos invader. Incus Maximal and Malleus Mundi: the Hammer and Anvil. We have dropped out of the immaterium to dock with a Mechanicus signum-station and recover personnel and valuable data. Though the great forges were lost, we are told that a flotilla, heavily laden with preserved knowledge and faithful servants of the Machine God, escaped the enemy. Not everywhere has been blessed with survivors, however. Across the rimward sectors there are reports of entire swathes of Imperial worlds silent in their destruction, populations rotting and cities aflame. Most alarming and admirable are the worlds denied to the invader by Imperial hands. There are reports of virus bombs deployed on the hive-world of Undine. A tragedy indeed, but one from which we might learn. Knowledge through sacrifice.'

The Imperial Fist looked back at the cocoons on the surgical slabs, the smashed yellow pauldrons of their plate still visible through the protective membrane.

'I have had my fill of questions, magos,' the Space Marine said. 'If you don't mind, I should like to be alone now.'

'Of course,' Urquidex said. 'If you would permit me one question more. For our records.'

'What is it?'

'What is your name?'

The Space Marine stared back out into the cold emptiness of the void.

'My name is Koorland, Second Captain,' the Imperial Fist told him. 'Wall-name... Slaughter.'

ABOUT THE AUTHOR

Rob Sanders is the author of 'The Serpent
Beneath', a novella that appeared in the New
York Times bestselling Horus Heresy anthology
The Primarchs. His other Black Library credits
include the Warhammer 40,000 titles *Adeptus
Mechanicus: Skitarius* and *Tech-Priest, Legion
of the Damned*, Atlas Infernal and Redemption
Corps and the audio drama The Path Forsaken.
He has also written the Warhammer Archaon
duology, Everchosen and Lord of Chaos, along
with many Quick Reads for the Horus Heresy
and Warhammer 40,000. He lives in the city
of Lincoln, UK.

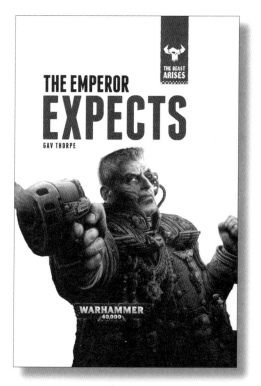

Extract from

The Emperor Expects

by Gav Thorpe

'Sir, we are registering an acceleration in the warp engine conduits,' said the other officer before Greydove could respond to the first. 'It looks as though our warp engines are coming online.'

'I gave no such order,' said Greydove.

'That would be Magos Laurentis, I believe.' Koorland's voice sounded loud and flat in the close confines. He looked at the sensor ensign. 'What range to the departing Adeptus Mechanicus vessel?'

'Twenty thousand miles and increasing,' the ensign replied automatically, responding to the raw authority of the Space Marine captain. The Naval officer glanced at Greydove for reassurance. 'Um, commander, we have received no signal to prepare for warp jump yet.'

'Lieutenant Greydove, please have your Navigator report to the bridge,' Koorland said quietly, standing beside the ship's captain.

'Why would I do that?'

'Because you have a change of orders, commander,' Koorland said.

The shrill whine of a warning siren cut off the lieutenant's response as red lights flashed across the bridge.

'Sir! Warp engines engaged!'

'Thirty seconds to translation,' barked a servitor just in front of Koorland and Greydove.

'What upon the Throne is that damned tech-priest doing?' the ship's commander demanded, turning on Koorland.

'A change of plans, commander. I am taking command of your ship.'

'You can't do that!'

'I already have. Magos Laurentis is activating the warp drive and I am currently standing on the bridge giving the orders. Which part of this scenario suggests to you, lieutenant, that I am not in complete control of the situation?'

Greydove opened his mouth dumbly a couple of times, searching for an answer. A desperate look creased his face.

'Don't make me assemble the armsmen, captain,' the lieutenant said, trying to sound stern.

'I will not think twice about killing your men,' Koorland said, uttering the words deliberately and slowly so that he would not be misunderstood. 'There is some chance that your men may succeed in pacifying me sufficiently for my return to Terra. They will not be able to do so without significant casualties.'

The Space Marine tried to reassure Greydove, taking the lieutenant's arm in a gentle grip.

'I intend no harm to this vessel or its crew.' Koorland

straightened but did not turn as he heard the distinctive snick of a holster being unfastened. He looked Greydove in the eye. 'Tell your ensign to secure his pistol, otherwise I will be forced to take it from him.'

Koorland heard an exhalation, saw a slight nod from Greydove and then using the dim reflection on one of the communication screens watched the officer fasten the holster once more. 'Good. We should avoid any rash actions at this moment.'

'Translation in five seconds,' warned the servitor monitoring the warp drive. 'Four... Three... Two... One...'

There was a lurch inside Koorland as reality and unreality momentarily occupied the same space. Every atom of his being fizzed for a few seconds and in the depths of his mind, somewhere near the base of his brain, a disturbing pressure forced its way into his thoughts.

After ten seconds, the sensation had passed.

'Translation successful,' the servitor announced, rather unnecessarily. Had translation not been successful everybody aboard would know about it – or be dead.

'I – I take it that you are not intending to travel to Terra?' said Greydove.

'That would be a waste of time, lieutenant. The Imperium is under threat and a suitable response is required. Honour demands that I continue the battle. I intend to rendezvous with my remaining brothers.'

'I don't understand. I was led to believe,' Greydove dropped his voice to a whisper and glanced cautiously at the other men, 'in greatest secrecy, that you were the last warrior of the Imperial Fists.'

'We call it the Last Wall protocol. In the event that Terra should be under grave threat, perhaps even fallen, the sons of Dorn will come together to deal with the matter as one.'

'But, excuse the question, if you are all dead, who is there to respond?'

'The Imperial Fists Chapter may have been destroyed, but the old Legion will remember.'

'The old Legion?' Greydove was horrified by the concept. 'But the Legions were broken apart by decree of the Emperor.'

'Not the Emperor,' snapped Koorland, more harshly than he had intended. He took a breath. 'By Imperial decree, yes, but it was not from the lips of the Emperor that the decree came. It matters not. The signal has been sent and I will wait for those who are fit to respond.'

'But if you are not going to Terra, where are we heading?'

'The last place our enemies would look for us. A place that lives long in the memory of the Legion. Tell your Navigator to chart a course for the Phall System.'